THE BROTHERHOOD OF THE PLAGUE

London 1665: mysteries and suspicious deaths

Thriller

Franco Nicoli

THE BROTHERHOOD OF THE PLAGUE

Prologue

In a 17th century London ravaged by plague and secrets, two men, Edward and Thomas, find themselves at the centre of a tangled web of intrigue, power and mystery. As the disease spreads unchecked, straining the very fabric of society, a secret brotherhood plots in the shadows, with plans beyond mere survival. But how do the stories of these two men intertwine with the greatest conspiracy of their time?

Through this narrative, immerse yourself in a historical London where every corner can hide a secret and every whisper can lead to truth or death. Follow Edward and Thomas in their struggle to unravel the mystery of the Brotherhood as they grapple with power, loyalty and loss.

But the story is not limited to them. Characters such as Lady Isabella, Lord Mayor and even King Charles II play crucial roles in this tangled web of fate and power. Their lives intertwine in unexpected ways, with decisions that have repercussions throughout the city and beyond.

THE BROTHERHOOD OF THE PLAGUE

London 1665

The Black Death

London, 1665, is a city at the heart of its golden century, but also a city on the brink of chaos. The bubonic plague, also known as the 'Black Death', makes its devastating appearance, turning the bustling metropolis into a place of desolation and terror.

Once crowded with merchants, carriages and citizens, the streets and alleys of London are now almost deserted. At regular intervals, along streets and alleys, house doors can be seen branded with large red crosses, a macabre signal that there are plague sufferers inside. "Lord have mercy on us" ("God have mercy on us") is a phrase written everywhere, a mute cry of despair. Every now and then, a wagon passes by, with men shouting "Bring out your dead!", collecting bodies to take to mass graves.

Trade has practically come to a standstill. Many shops are closed and the once thriving markets are now silent and empty.

THE BROTHERHOOD OF THE PLAGUE

The city's economy is on its knees, with people fleeing or hiding in their homes.

Distrust reigns supreme. Lifelong neighbours avoid each other, fearing infection. Whole families are confined to their homes, often dying together. Doctors, or those who pretend to be, roam the streets with beak-shaped masks filled with herbs, believing that this protects them from the disease. Many take advantage of the situation, selling false cures and amulets.

Many nobles and wealthy citizens abandoned the city to take refuge in their country estates, far from disease. Their large houses in central London remain closed and deserted.

Although many churches are closed for fear of contagion, some remain open, with preachers proclaiming the plague as divine retribution for the sins of the city. Groups of penitents gather, praying and scourging themselves hoping for redemption.

There is a constant atmosphere of fear. People cover their faces with handkerchiefs or cloths, hoping to avoid contagion. Many families have planted aromatic flowers such as lavender or rosemary in front of their houses, hoping that their scent will keep the disease away.

In this desolate scenario, life goes on anyway, with small acts of kindness, courage and determination. While many see the plague as an inevitable death sentence, others seek solutions, offering help and hope to the less fortunate.

THE BROTHERHOOD OF THE PLAGUE

London in 1665 is a city transformed, a place where tragedy and humanity intertwine in a dramatic ballet of survival.

Deserted London

The London skyline, once thickly dotted with smoking chimneys and noisy merchants, was now a ghostly landscape. The Thames, which once flowed under the tumultuous bustle of barges and rowing boats, was now calm and silent, its billows moving lazily under a leaden sky.

The air was cold, an icy wind blew in from the north, sweeping through the deserted streets, blowing shop signs and hissing through the narrow alleys. This wind carried with it an acrid smell, a mixture of fire, disinfectant and death. Occasionally, the wind also carried the distant wail of someone, or the cry of an infant. But they were sporadic sounds, almost like echoes of a distant past.

On many house doors, heavy red crosses had been painted, along with the inscription: 'God have mercy on us'. Behind those doors, life and death were in a continuous dance. But from the street, nothing could be seen or heard. Only those crosses, like mute cries, spoke of the horror hidden inside.

THE BROTHERHOOD OF THE PLAGUE

In one of the wider streets, near a square, there was a fountain. At one time, it was a meeting place where women gathered to discuss the latest news, children played and men drank and chatted. Now, the fountain was dry and an almost sacred silence reigned around it.

From the square, a tall tower could be seen, the bell tower of a church. The bells, however, were no longer ringing. Beside them, a black flag waved slowly, a monitor and a symbol of the desolation that had befallen the city.

Next to the fountain, sitting on a bench, was an old man. He had a long white beard and wore threadbare clothes. He held an old violin in his hands. After looking into the distance, as if searching for something or someone, he began to play. The notes were melancholic, but surprisingly beautiful, and they echoed in the deserted square.

From a side alley, a young woman appeared with a basket under her arm. Her black hair was pulled back into a bun and she was wearing a simple but clean dress. She stopped when she heard music and approached the man slowly.

"Why are you playing, old man? At a time like this?" he asked, his voice soft but full of curiosity.

The old man looked up, his eyes were a deep blue, almost transparent. "Music," he replied in a rough voice, "is the last refuge when all else seems lost. It reminds me that there was a time, before all this, and that perhaps there will be a time afterwards."

The young woman nodded slowly, then, with a sudden gesture, opened the basket and pulled out a small loaf of bread. "For you," she said, "for your music."

The old man, surprised, took the bread with trembling hands. "Thank you," he whispered. "In these times, even a small gesture can make a difference."

The young woman smiled sadly. "Perhaps one day, when all this is over, we can gather here, in the square, and dance again to the sound of your music."

"That would be nice," replied the old man, "but now, let me play for you." And so, in a desolate and silent London, the old fiddler played, and for a brief moment, the square seemed to come back to life.

The image slowly recedes, showing once again the vastness of the desolation, the empty streets and the marked houses. But at the heart of that desolation, there was still life, still hope. And that hope lay in small human interactions, in acts of kindness, in the beauty of music.

THE BROTHERHOOD OF THE PLAGUE

Twenty suspects

Introduction to Edward

Edward Fairfax's house was tucked away in a quiet corner of London, close to the river. It was a two-storey building, built of grey stone and red brick. The interior was humble but well maintained, with wooden floors and walls decorated with paintings of serene landscapes.

In his bedroom, the first ray of morning light filtered through the heavy green curtains, revealing a simple but uncluttered room. A large bed with white linen sheets, an oak dresser and a desk full of papers and medical instruments.

Edward sat on the edge of the bed, his face marked by fatigue and anxiety. His hair was black, now marked by a few strands of silver, and his eyes were a deep blue, shining with determination at that moment. He wore a white shirt and was slowly buttoning his brown velvet waistcoat.

As he dressed, his thoughts raced. He thought of his city, London, the plague, his patients. He thought of the faces of those he had tried to save and those he had lost. And every image, every memory, weighed on his heart like a boulder.

On the other side of the room, on a table, was a sack of rough canvas. Edward walked over to it and began to fill it carefully. Glass bottles with handwritten labels: 'Tincture of opium', 'Zinc sulphate', 'Belladonna extract'. Besides the medicines, he put some bandages, a pair of pliers and a small scalpel in the bag.

As he worked, the door of the room slowly opened and a young woman peeped in. It was Mary, his servant, a girl with blond hair and green eyes. "Sir, I have prepared breakfast," she said in a shy voice.

Edward looked up and offered her a reassuring smile. "Thank you, Mary. I'll be down in a bit."

The girl nodded and was about to close the door when Edward stopped her. "Mary, did you hear anything during the night? Screaming, crying?"

Mary hesitated for a moment. "I heard Mrs Thompson crying across the street. I think her husband is..."

Edward nodded. "I know, I visited him yesterday. There was nothing I could do."

Mary's face clouded with sadness. 'It is so difficult, sir. Every day we lose someone. I wonder when it will end."

Edward approached her and took her by the shoulders. "We must have faith, Mary. And do our best to help those we can." He looked into her eyes. "And you, how are you?"

Mary tried to smile. "I'm fine, sir. Just a little tired."

Edward nodded, concerned. "If you feel sick, you have to tell me right away. Understand?"

The girl answered firmly. "I promise."

Edward finished filling the sack and headed for the door. "I'll be out for most of the day. If anything happens, you know where to find me."

Mary nodded. "Be careful, sir."

Edward offered her one last reassuring smile and left the room. As he descended the stairs, thoughts of the gravity of the situation came flooding back. But he knew that he had to go on, that he had to do his best to save as many lives as possible. It was his duty, his mission. And he would not stop as long as he had an ounce of strength in his body.

THE BROTHERHOOD OF THE PLAGUE

First Visit

The streets of London, once lively and noisy, were now as silent as a graveyard. Edward walked at a brisk pace, his figure silhouetted against the dark horizon of the city, his canvas sack slung over his shoulder. From time to time he looked up at the windows of the houses, noticing the drawn curtains and tightly closed doors. But what disturbed him most were the red crosses, cruelly painted on the doors, like infected scars on a sick body.

Suddenly, he turned into a narrow, lesser-known alley, trying to avoid the main streets. After a few minutes, he stopped in front of a red-brick house, modest but well-kept. There were no red cross marks on the door, a promising sign.

Edward knocked three times, waiting with his heart in his throat. After a long silence, a series of locks clicked and the door slowly opened, revealing a woman in her forties, with dark hair pulled back into a bun and large, frightened eyes. Behind her, in the shadows, the faces of two children could be made out.

"Who are you?" asked the woman in a trembling voice.

"I am Dr Edward Fairfax," he replied, showing his bag of medicines. "I heard you might need some help."

The woman watched him for a moment, then, with a sigh of relief, let him in. "Please come in. My husband is very ill."

The house was dark and quiet, with the curtains drawn and the furniture covered with sheets. Edward followed the woman into a small room downstairs, where a man lay on a bed, covered in sweat and shivering.

"John started being sick three days ago," the woman explained, with tears in her eyes. "He has a high fever and pains everywhere."

Edward approached the bed, observing the patient with expert eyes. He touched the man's forehead, feeling the feverish heat. Then he took a small torch and illuminated his eyes, noting the dilation of the pupils.

After examining John for a few minutes, Edward turned to the woman. "It is not the plague," he said in a calm voice. "But he does have a serious infection. I have to give him some medicine and keep him under observation."

The woman nodded, relieved. "Thank you, doctor. We will do whatever you ask."

Edward started to prepare a solution from one of his bottles, mixing different ingredients in a bowl. As he worked, one of the children, a boy of about ten with blond hair and curious eyes, approached.

"You are a real doctor?" asked the child.

Edward smiled. "Yes, I am. And who are you?"

"My name is Robert," replied the little boy. "Can you really help my father?"

Edward put a hand on the boy's shoulder. "I will do my best. And you must be strong for your mother and sister."

The child nodded, trying to hold back tears. "I will be, I promise."

After administering the medicine to John, Edward sat beside the bed, observing him carefully. His fever slowly began to drop and the man seemed more relaxed.

"Many thanks, doctor," whispered the woman, holding her husband's hand. "I don't know how we can ever repay you."

Edward offered her a sympathetic smile. 'Don't worry about that. The important thing is that your husband recovers. And remember to keep him warm and give him plenty of water."

The woman nodded, grateful. "I will, thank you again."

Edward stood up, putting his tools away. "I'll check back in a few days. In the meantime, if you need anything, you know where to find me."

The family accompanied him to the door, thanking him profusely. As Edward stepped out into the deserted street, he heard a small voice behind him. It was Robert, his eyes shining.

"You are a hero, doctor," said the child. "Thank you for saving my father."

Edward smiled at him, touched. "Just doing my job. But thank you for your words."

And with those words of hope and gratitude, Edward continued on his way home.

Rumours and Gossip

The warm London afternoon sun shone faintly through a curtain of thick, grey fog. As soon as Edward stepped outside the house, the dull sound of his shoes on the cobblestones seemed to break the impenetrable silence of the street. The atmosphere was charged, as if fear and tension were coursing through the air.

As he advanced along the pavement, Edward's ear caught a whisper coming from a house not far away. He stopped for a moment, trying to locate the source of the sound. The whisper came from an open window on the first floor, where two women, partially hidden by heavy velvet curtains, were deep in furtive conversation.

"I told you, Agatha," whispered one, "I saw the cross on the Williams' door, but I don't trust it. They say their bodies had no plague marks."

The other woman's voice, more hoarse and cracked, replied: 'And what do you suggest, Mabel? That there was some witchcraft? Don't talk nonsense!"

Edward casually leaned against the wall of a nearby house, trying to listen inconspicuously.

Mabel continued, her voice now filled with concern: "I'm not saying it's witchcraft, but I heard that they didn't have the typical boils of the disease. It was as if something or someone had... poisoned or cursed them."

Agatha sighed heavily. "In these times, rumours run fast, and fear makes people say the strangest things. Maybe it was just a different form of the disease."

Edward felt his heart pounding in his chest. Mabel's words awakened in him a growing suspicion, fuelled by his recent discovery in the Williams' house. He decided to intervene.

"Good afternoon, sir," he said, looking up at the window. "I apologise for the intrusion, but I couldn't help but overhear what you were talking about. I am Dr Edward Fairfax."

The women retreated abruptly behind the curtain, but shortly afterwards Mabel, a burly woman with grey hair and a wrinkled face, cautiously poked her head out. "What do you want, doctor?"

Edward tried to sound as reassuring as possible. "I was interested in what you were saying about the Williams family. I visited their home a short while ago and noticed some... inconsistencies."

Agatha, a slim woman with black hair tied in a braid, joined Mabel at the window, her dark eyes filled with curiosity. "What do you mean, doctor?"

Edward hesitated for a moment, searching for the right words. "The bodies I examined did not seem to have the typical symptoms of plague. I was curious if you had heard or seen anything unusual."

Mabel and Agatha exchanged a look. "We... we have only heard rumours, Doctor," said Mabel, clearly reluctant to speak. "But in times like these, who is to say what is true and what is not?"

Edward nodded slowly. "I understand. I thank you for your time. If you hear or see anything strange, please inform me."

The women nodded, and the window slowly closed, leaving Edward alone with his thoughts. His mind was working at full tilt, trying to put the pieces of the puzzle together.

"Something doesn't add up," he muttered to himself as he walked towards the Williams' house, determined to unravel the mystery surrounding those mysterious deaths.

THE BROTHERHOOD OF THE PLAGUE

Arrival at the House of Williams

The neighbourhood in which the Williams' house was located was one of the most prestigious in London. The houses were stately, with ornate stone facades, impressive windows and manicured gardens. The Williams' house was no exception. It stood proudly in the middle of a street, but its grandeur was overshadowed by the red cross on the door, a symbol of death and illness.

The late afternoon light cast eerie shadows along the paved driveway leading to the entrance of the residence. There was no sign of life outside, only the distant song of a bird and the rustling of leaves stirred by the wind created an unreal atmosphere.

Edward stopped in front of the large oak door, his heart throbbing with a mixture of trepidation and determination. He knocked three times, echoing in the depths of the house. He waited, but there was no answer.

"Well, Edward," he muttered to himself, "it looks like you'll have to do some investigating on your own."

Turning the handle, the door opened with a sinister creak. The interior was shrouded in half-light, only a few faint rays of light filtered through the heavy, closed curtains. The air inside was stagnant and heavy, laden with a metallic odour, familiar to Edward: the smell of blood.

Proceeding cautiously, Edward entered a large living room. Fine furniture, portraits of ancestors and a large stone fireplace dominated the room. In the centre, a large mahogany table was set as if the family was ready to dine, but the plates and cutlery were covered in dust, and the food was rotten.

"It seems as if time had stopped," Edward murmured, examining the details of the room.

As he proceeded, a noise from above caught his attention. A series of light footsteps, perhaps of a child or a woman, followed by a barely audible whisper. Edward decided to follow the sound, hoping to find some survivors.

He climbed the marble stairs, whose balustrades were decorated with intricate carvings. On the first floor, a long corridor stretched before him, with closed doors on both sides. He walked towards the end of the corridor, where the whispering came from.

Arriving at a particular door, he noticed that it was ajar. Pushing slightly, the door opened onto a bedroom. Inside, a young woman sat on the edge of the bed, dressed in a white dress, her long black hair flowed over her shoulders and she seemed to be cradling something in her arms.

Edward stepped forward. "Miss? I am Dr Edward Fairfax. May I help you?"

The woman slowly lifted her gaze, revealing deep, terrified eyes. "I am Eleanor, the Williams' youngest daughter," she replied in a trembling voice. "I hid my brother here, hoping the disease would not reach him."

Edward approached, noticing that what Eleanor was cradling were the blankets wrapped around a small, lifeless body. "I am deeply sorry, Miss Eleanor. Is there anything I can do for you?"

Eleanor seemed about to collapse, but her words were firm: 'Doctor, my father and mother died in a strange way. They had no signs of the plague. And I'm afraid there's something more sinister at play."

Edward nodded gravely. "I suspected as much. Will you allow me to examine the bodies?"

Eleanor pointed to a door on the opposite side of the room. "I'm in the next room."

As Edward headed for that door, he knew he was about to enter a world of mystery and danger, but he was determined to discover the truth behind the tragic death of the Williams family.

Macabre Discovery

Edward opened the door Eleanor had pointed out to him, revealing a room bathed in a cold, bluish light. The room, which must have once been an elegant dining room, had been transformed into a place of death.

Inside, the floor was littered with the bodies of members of the Williams family. The father, Lord Harold, lay by the fireplace, his formal dress immaculate were it not for the dark stains that had formed around his wounds. His mother, Lady Agatha, was lying not far away, still in her evening dress, a fan of white feathers beside her. The other bodies evidently belonged to the younger members of the family, still dressed in their party clothes.

The table in the centre of the room had been overturned, the candlesticks had fallen and the candles were out. On the floor, a few broken plates and spilled wine glasses suggested a fight. Yet what struck Edward most was not the scene of chaos, but rather a detail: the bodies did not have the typical plague boils. No black spots, no obvious swelling.

He approached cautiously, wearing leather gloves and a cloth mask for protection. He lowered himself beside the body of Lord Harold, examining the pale skin and purple lips. The wounds looked strange, not made by a blade or weapon, but rather as if something had sucked the life out of him.

"What happened to you, Lord Harold?" murmured Edward, as he inspected the body.

Behind him, the door swung open. Eleanor stood on the threshold, her eyes fixed on the figures lying on the floor. "I didn't have the courage to come in here after I found them," she said in a trembling voice.

Edward stood up, directing his gaze at her. "Eleanor, these wounds... they weren't made by a man. Or by an animal I know."

Eleanor nodded, her face as pale as a ghost. "I knew it. I knew it wasn't the plague."

He slowly approached his mother's body, picking up the feather fan and clasping it in his hands. "It was the night of our annual masquerade ball," she began. "My father had invited many guests. But there was a stranger, with a black mask and cold eyes. After he left, the family retreated here to discuss him. And then... then I don't remember. I woke up in my bed and found everything like this."

Edward watched her, looking for signs of lies or insincerity, but all he saw was genuine pain and terror. "We have to figure out what or who did this. If it's a murderer or something . supernatural."

Eleanor looked into his eyes, her determination working its way through the tears. "I will help you. I will do anything that can help you. I owe it to their memory."

Edward understood. "First, we have to make sure the bodies are treated with respect. Then we will begin our investigation."

As he spoke, a cold breeze blew through the room, shifting the curtains and creating ghostly shadows. Both felt a chill, as if they were being watched.

"Eleanor," Edward said in a low voice, "I think our search has just begun."

The Clue

The silence in the hall was oppressive. Every now and then, a ticking came from the grandfather clock on the wall, its sound breaking the silence like a hammer. Eleanor still stood beside Edward, her hands clutching the feather fan, and her eyes, swollen with tears, looked at his face, searching for an answer, an explanation.

Edward was bent over Lady Agatha's body, his attentive and meticulous gaze moving from side to side, searching for any clue that might provide an explanation for those mysterious deaths. Lady Agatha's dress was made of blue silk, with fine silver wefts drawing intricate spirals on the fabric. There were no visible signs of struggle or violence on her dress.

As his gaze ran down the side of Lady Agatha's neck, he noticed something strange. Behind her right ear, hidden by curls of dark hair, was a small incision. It looked like a surgical cut, precise and clean.

"Eleanor," he said slowly, "come and see this."

Eleanor approached, her gaze following Edward's. "What... what is it?"

Edward took a pair of tweezers from his medical bag and gently moved Lady Agatha's hair to better reveal the incision. "I don't know. But it's too precise to have been made in a moment of panic or during a fight."

With a deep breath, Edward moved towards Lord Harold's body and examined behind his ear. The same small incision was there. One by one, Edward checked all the bodies in the room, and every single family member had the same incision.

Eleanor murmured, "It's like a mark. A mark."

Edward nodded. "Or maybe something was inserted or removed from there. But why?"

Eleanor turned away from the bodies, her eyes staring into the void, as if trying to put the pieces of a jigsaw puzzle together. "That man, the stranger with the black mask.... Could it be him?"

Edward stood up and approached Eleanor, his hands gently gripping her by the shoulders. "We cannot jump to hasty conclusions. But certainly, this engraving is the first real clue we have."

At that moment, a sound came from outside the house. The sound of hurried footsteps, confused voices. Eleanor looked out of the window and saw a group of people with torches, approaching the entrance to the residence.

"What's going on?" asked Edward, reaching out to her.

Eleanor stepped back from the window, her face pale. "It's the city guard. They must have heard about the deaths here."

Edward looked at the bodies, then back at Eleanor. "We can't let them in now. Not until we've solved this mystery."

Eleanor nodded, determined. "I have a secret room, where we can hide the bodies. But we must hurry."

As Eleanor guided Edward to the secret room, they both knew in their hearts that the night had just begun, and that the real danger was about to come.

Doubts and Theories

In the semi-darkness of the secret room, the faint glow of candles illuminated dim baroque figures painted on the walls, their expressions seeming to change as the flames swung. Eleanor had placed several candles around the room to give them a decent view as they worked. The floor was cold under the tiles, and moisture was palpable in the air.

Edward was sitting in an antique armchair, his gaze fixed on the floor. His mind was in turmoil. The buzz of questions nagged at him like an inextricable riddle. The presence of that incision behind each victim's ear gave him chills down his spine.

Eleanor looked at him as he moved nervously. "Edward?" she said in a gentle tone, trying to break his trance. "Are you OK?"

He lifted his gaze, his piercing eyes fixed on hers. 'I'm wondering what could have caused those deaths. The carving... it doesn't look like a simple mark. But rather an access point."

Eleanor approached him slowly. "Access point? To what?"

Edward hesitated a moment, 'It could be that something was injected or removed from there. A poison, perhaps? But why do such a complicated thing when there are much simpler ways to poison someone?"

Eleanor sat in a nearby armchair, pondering Edward's words. 'What if it's not a poison? What if it's something . different? Something none of us have ever seen or heard of before?"

Edward nodded, contemplating the idea. 'You're right, we have to consider all possibilities. But what concerns me most is the motive. Why would someone want to kill your family in this elaborate way?"

Eleanor lowered her eyes, searching the depths of her memory. "I cannot think of any enemy who could have done such a thing. But that mysterious visitor, the man in the black mask... he could be the key to all this."

Edward looked at her, his eyes were full of compassion. "We have to find out who he was. We need to talk to all the guests who were present that night. One of them might have recognised him or might know something."

Eleanor nodded, determined. "You are right. But first, we must make sure the bodies stay safe here. We can't risk the city guard finding them."

Edward stood up, placing a reassuring hand on Eleanor's shoulder. "We'll take care of everything, Eleanor. We'll find who did this and bring them to justice."

The resoluteness in his eyes gave her a glimmer of hope. With a deep breath, Eleanor said, "Let us begin. The night is not over yet and there is much work to be done."

As they prepared to leave the secret room, both knew that the road ahead would be long and dangerous. But both were determined to discover the truth, whatever it was.

THE BROTHERHOOD OF THE PLAGUE

Search for Confirmations

With the atmosphere of the secret room still on them, Edward and Eleanor ventured into the rest of the house. Footsteps echoed on the tiles, and each echo seemed to amplify their loneliness. The cloth-covered furniture created ghostly silhouettes in the half-darkened rooms, while candlelight produced shadows that moved across the walls like restless spirits.

"This is the library," Eleanor murmured, pushing open a heavy oak door. The room revealed itself before them, filled with shelves overflowing with ancient volumes, many of them covered in dust. "If there is any clue or any record that might help you, you would find it here."

Edward nodded, starting to examine the titles on the nearest shelf. As he moved from shelf to shelf, his eyes caught something unusual on the fireplace. A partially burnt letter lay among the still warm remains of wood. He approached it cautiously, carefully extracting the fragment of paper with tongs.

Eleanor, seeing Edward's attention, approached. "What have you found?"

Edward studied the letter, trying to decipher the words written in elegant but fast handwriting. "It is not completely legible because of the fire, but I can do my best." He read aloud: "...must take place. The secret meeting... in the moonlight... don't fail, Reginald..."

"Reginald?" Eleanor looked puzzled. "I don't know any Reginalds. And this secret meeting, what could it be about?"

Edward carefully folded the letter fragment, placing it in an inside pocket of his jacket. 'Could it be related to the deaths? Or maybe it's just a coincidence. But we must investigate further."

As they explored the library further, Eleanor approached a drawer hidden under a massive desk. She slowly opened it, revealing a diary. "This was my father's," she said softly. "Perhaps it might contain some information."

Edward picked up the diary, leafing through it carefully. The pages contained notes, accounts and personal considerations, but one entry caught his attention. It was dated a few days before the tragedy: "I received an unexpected visitor today. A masked man, who introduced himself as Reginald. He says he has crucial information for me, but wants to meet me in secret. I don't know whether to trust him..."

Eleanor approached, reading the diary entry. "My father never spoke of this. Who could this Reginald be?"

Edward closed the diary, looking at Eleanor. 'I don't know. But now we have a name and a possible link to the tragedy. We have to find out who this Reginald is and what role he played in all this."

Both felt the weight of the situation. The house, with its secrets and mysteries, seemed to envelop them like a fog. But they knew they had to keep searching, to honour the memory of the dead and to find justice.

"Let's keep looking," Eleanor said, determined. "Every corner of this house could hide another clue."

Edward nodded, and together, they went further into the house, determined to unravel the mystery surrounding them, but finding no other clues. Edward decided it was time to leave, told Eleanor to stay hidden and to avoid letting on that anyone was home.

The wind outside had a plaintive tone, caressing the Williams' mansion like a lament of a lost soul. The noises of the city in agony were distant and muffled. The black clouds in the sky threatened rain, but Edward had much bigger worries to deal with.

As he made his way to the main exit, the heavy wooden door suddenly opened, letting in a wave of cold air. In front of him stood four city guards, recognisable by their leather helmets and thick vests, looking at the dwelling with eyes full of fear and suspicion.

"Hey, you!" thundered one of the guards, pointing at Edward. "What are you doing here?"

Edward paused, trying to keep calm. "I am Dr Fairfax," he said, showing his medical bag. "I'm here to help. I heard about some strange deaths in this house and wanted to investigate."

The guards exchanged uncertain glances. One of them, a short, stocky man with a shaggy beard, approached. "The plague is ravaging the city, doctor. It is not wise to walk around, especially in houses like this."

Edward nodded, 'I know, but it is my duty to help where I can. And I have found something unusual here. There is something darker and more sinister behind these deaths."

The guard raised an eyebrow, "What do you mean?"

Before Edward could reply, another guard, a thin one with a long moustache, interrupted, "We have been ordered to check all houses with red crosses and make sure the dead are buried. We cannot allow the plague to spread any further."

Edward put his hand on his chest, 'I assure you, what I have discovered here could change everything. But I need more time to investigate. Please give science the opportunity to unveil the truth."

The guards consulted each other with glances and whispers. The stocky guard finally said, "All right, doctor. But we don't have much time. This city is dying and we cannot allow delays."

"I promise you," Edward said, his voice firm and confident, "that I will find out what is going on. But I need you to do me a favour."

The subtle guard raised an eyebrow, "And which one would that be?"

Edward hesitated for a moment, then said, 'Stop people from coming here. If news of the deaths spreads, it could cause panic. Also, if my theories are correct, whoever did this might come back."

The stocky guard scratched his beard, "Fine. But know that if you do not find answers, we will have to do what is necessary to protect the city."

Edward nodded, "I know. And I am grateful for your understanding."

With one last glance at the house, Edward walked away, determined to unravel the mystery within its walls. The guards watched him go, hoping his words were true and that he could find a solution to this nightmare.

THE BROTHERHOOD OF THE PLAGUE

The Sign of the Assassin

Obsession

The smell of leather and old paper permeated the air of Edward Fairfax's workshop. Shelves covered with books and bottles of various sizes and colours gave the place an atmosphere of mystery. A single oil lamp, with its flickering flame, lit the room, casting shadows on the bare brick walls.

Edward, with messy hair and a few days old beard, was sitting at his massive oak table. With a magnifying glass in his hand, he carefully studied a detailed sketch of a human ear. On the surface of the drawing, he had highlighted a small incision located exactly behind the earlobe. Beside him, a pile of reports and notes rose ominously, ready to collapse at any moment. "It doesn't make sense..." he muttered to himself, taking another sketch and comparing it with the first.

The shadows, dancing on the paper, seemed to agree with him, whispering their hidden secrets. From time to time, Edward would pause, focusing on a note or a particular detail, and then return to immerse himself in his thoughts.

An inkwell was upturned on a corner of the table, a few drops of ink having stained the wooden surface. Evidently, in a moment of frustration or realisation, Edward had bumped the container.

The door to the laboratory creaked slightly, barely opening. A soft but concerned female voice asked, "Edward? May I come in?"

Edward looked up, as if he had been pulled out of a trance. 'Oh, Eliza, it's you. Sorry, I was lost in my thoughts. What is it?"

Eliza, a young woman with brown hair pulled back into a bun and expressive eyes, cautiously entered. 'I was just passing by and noticed the light. You haven't slept for days, Edward. This... obsession is consuming you."

Edward sighed, running a hand wearily over his face. 'I know, Eliza, but I feel I'm close to a breakthrough. These carvings... they're not random. There must be a reason."

Eliza approached, observing the splashes on the table. "But they are only ears, Edward. What could they reveal to you?"

Edward looked at her intently, almost trying to convey to her the gravity of his discovery. "They are not *just* ears. They are the sign of something bigger, something dark. And I intend to find out what."

Eliza took Edward's hand between her own. "Please be careful. I don't want to lose you to this... obsession."

Edward smiled weakly, squeezing Eliza's hand. "I promise I will be careful. But I must get to the bottom of this mystery."

With a look of sadness and concern, Eliza slowly withdrew, leaving Edward to his sketches and mysteries.

The Unexpected Visit

The candles in Edward's study were slowly burning out, and the flame cast grotesque shadows on the brick walls. With each passing hour, the pile of notes and drawings on the table grew, like a mute testimony to Edward's fervent research. Every now and then, the silence was interrupted by the scrape of his pen or a sigh of frustration.

But that silence was suddenly interrupted when the study door was thrown wide open. Thomas, a burly man with raven hair and a scar across his left cheek, burst into the room, sending a gust of cold air flying.

"For God's sake, Edward!" exclaimed Thomas, looking around with a worried expression. "Look, I know you're going through a tough time, but you're really overreacting."

Edward looked up, watching his friend's break-in with surprise. "Thomas, what are you doing here? I wasn't expecting you."

Thomas approached the table, examining the mass of papers. "And this?" he asked, raising an eyebrow, "Looks like the work of a madman."

Edward straightened up, defensively. 'I'm not crazy, Thomas. There is a pattern here. And something terribly wrong is happening in this town."

Thomas took one of the sketches, examining it carefully. "Ears?" he asked, a little puzzled. "Are you having sleepless nights over ears?"

Edward took the drawing from Thomas's hands, pointing to the incision behind his ear. "Look here. Do you see this engraving? It's not a sign of the plague. It's too precise, too... intentional."

Thomas shrugged, still sceptical. "It could be a coincidence. An accidental wound."

Edward shook his head vigorously. 'No, I've seen it in too many bodies. And not just in the bodies of those who died of the plague, but in those who looked... intact. Someone is killing these people, and this carving is their signature."

Thomas's face became serious. "Are you sure about this? Don't you just want to find a culprit for all the deaths?"

Edward sighed, feeling tired and overwhelmed. "I know, it sounds crazy. But I can't ignore what I see. And I feel like I'm close to a breakthrough."

Thomas looked at his friend, concern in his eyes. 'Edward, you are my friend. If you really believe there is a killer out there, I will help you. But you must promise me to take a break. This obsession is destroying you."

Edward looked at Thomas with gratitude in his eyes. "Thank you, Thomas. But I need to get to the bottom of this conundrum. For all the victims. And for myself."

Thomas nodded slowly. "Good. Then let's get started. But first, let's get out of this study and have a cup of tea. It will all seem less oppressive afterwards."

Edward laughed slightly, accepting his friend's outstretched hand. "Alright, a break. But then, back to work."

As the two left the studio, the oppressive atmosphere seemed to ease slightly, as if the shared determination had rekindled a spark of hope amidst the darkness.

Edward's small kitchen was lit by the warm glow of candles. A cup of hot tea smoked on a small table, and the delicate aroma of tea mixed with the fragrance of the woods in the room gave a sense of warmth and cosiness. Despite the relaxed atmosphere, the air was tense.

Thomas, sitting opposite Edward, rubbed his temple, trying to absorb the information presented to him. "Alright, Edward," he began, "so you're saying that someone is killing these people and making it look like they died from the plague? That's a bold theory. Do you have any proof?"

Edward, taking a deep breath before starting. 'Look, I know how crazy this sounds, but I can't ignore what I saw. Every time I examine one of those bodies, I always find the same incision behind the ear. It's too precise, too clean to be a mere coincidence."

Thomas took a sip of tea, his eyes intensely scanning Edward. "You said these people seemed... untouched. What do you mean by that?"

Edward put his cup aside and placed his hands on the table. 'Most plague victims show visible symptoms, such as boils and black spots on the skin. But these bodies... They looked almost... immaculate. As if they had been killed by something completely different."

Thomas wrinkled his forehead, 'So why would anyone do such a thing? Kill people and then make them look like they died of the plague? It doesn't make sense."

Edward hesitated for a moment. 'I don't know yet. But that's why I need your help, Thomas. If there really is a killer out there, I must stop him before he kills again."

Thomas put down his cup and leaned back in his chair. 'If what you say is true, we are facing something very dangerous. And if someone is really doing what you suspect, there must be a reason. We must find out who it is and why he is doing this."

Edward nodded vigorously. 'Exactly. And to do that, we have to carefully examine all the clues. Every detail could be crucial."

Thomas got up from his chair. "All right, Edward. I'm with you. We'll start tomorrow, visit some of the houses where you noticed these... engravings."

Edward smiled, finally feeling less alone in this struggle. "Thank you, Thomas. With your insight and my medical know-how, I'm sure we can get to the bottom of this mystery."

Edward and Thomas had moved to the most secluded corner of Edward's workshop, where a wall of books gave a sense of solemnity and reflection. Candlelight danced on the pages of the old books, creating an atmosphere of stillness and recollection. Thomas ran a hand over his beard, reflecting. "Edward, what you have told me brought to mind an incident that occurred during one of my missions to the continent."

Edward, sitting in the wooden chair, leaned forward, interested. "Really? Tell me about it."

"During my military career, we faced a particular enemy," Thomas began. "A group of assassins who used a similar technique to mark their targets. A small incision behind the ear, almost like a mark. It was a sign to other members that that target had been 'taken'."

Edward straightened up, surprised. "Are you serious? That changes everything!"

Thomas nodded slowly. "Yes. But the question is, why would someone in London do the same thing? Who could have learned this technique and, more importantly, why does he use it?"

There was a moment of silence as the two men assimilated the information. Then Edward asked, "Do you have any idea who might be behind this?"

Thomas hesitated, "I don't want to make hasty assumptions, but it could be an old enemy... or someone who has studied military tactics and adapted them for their own sinister purposes here in London."

Edward reflected on what Thomas had just shared. "You said the carving was a mark.... Is there a possibility that these people were marked for some reason? And if so, what?"

"During my mission," Thomas said, "engraving was a way of communicating between members of the group. It was a way to say, 'This target is mine. Don't interfere.' But here, it could mean something completely different."

Edward jotted some notes in his notebook, then looked up at Thomas. "You are right. We need to understand the motive

THE BROTHERHOOD OF THE PLAGUE

behind this engraving. Thomas, have you noticed any connection between the victims? Perhaps a motive, a link that might give us a lead?"

Thomas stood up and started pacing back and forth, reflecting. "I cannot say for sure, but there was a common element among some of the victims I met. Many were merchants or had ties to the trade."

Edward nodded slowly. "Interesting... could there be an economic motive behind this? An attempt to control trade during this time of crisis?"

Thomas paused, looking at Edward. 'It could be. But we have to go deeper, look for other connections, other clues. It's the only way to get closer to the truth."

Edward stood up and offered his hand to Thomas. "You are right. Thank you for sharing this information with me. Every piece of the puzzle helps us get closer to the solution."

Thomas shook Edward's hand. "We will find who is behind this, Edward. And we will bring him to justice."

THE BROTHERHOOD OF THE PLAGUE

The Link

Edward's laboratory was a refuge from the outside, but on this particular night, it looked like a ship of knowledge in a sea of uncertainty. In the centre, a large oak desk was covered with reports, letters and newspapers. A few candles illuminated the room with a dim, flickering light, casting shadows on the book-lined walls.

Edward was standing in front of the desk, his forehead wrinkled in a grimace of concentration as he tried to establish a pattern among the victims. Thomas, seated in a straight-backed wooden chair, quickly flipped through a register of births and deaths.

'Something is wrong, Thomas,' Edward said, running a hand nervously through his hair. "These victims... they're not the usual people you'd expect to find stricken by the plague. They are wealthy merchants, nobles, influential citizens."

Thomas looked up, his grey eyes shining under the candlelight. 'You are right. And, as we discussed earlier, they do not appear to have died from the plague. This assassin or assassins are targeting a certain type of victim. But why?"

Edward took one of the reports and began to read aloud: 'Lord Alistair, dead last week, wealthy merchant and member of the City Council. Lady Margaret, one of the richest women in London, found dead in her residence three days ago...'

As Edward continued listing the victims, Thomas reflected aloud: "I don't see any obvious reason to kill these people unless there is a political or financial movement. They could be victims of some kind of plot to destabilise the city or the economy."

Edward paused, looking at his friend. "Are you suggesting that someone might want to take advantage of the panic caused by the plague to take control? To consolidate power?"

Thomas nodded slowly. 'That might make sense. London high society is a web of power and influence. If someone were able to eliminate the right people, they might find a way to control the strands."

"My God," whispered Edward, putting the report down. "If what you say is true, then we are facing a conspiracy of unthinkable proportions. And the killer may have influential allies."

The two men exchanged a meaningful glance. Thomas stood up, putting on his jacket. "We have to find out who is behind this. And we have to do it quickly."

Edward nodded decisively. "We will start by interviewing the families of the victims, trying to find a connection. Any little detail might help us solve this mystery." "I'll take care of the legal part," Thomas said. "I'll interview some of my contacts in the police. See if they've heard anything."

THE BROTHERHOOD OF THE PLAGUE

Action Plan

The rain gently tapped against the laboratory windows, a constant hum echoing through the room. As the candlelight reflected off the drops of water, the room exuded an aura of mystery.

Edward was leaning against his desk, the arms of his sleeves rolled up, exposing his calloused hands and the scars of his years of medical practice. Thomas, on the other hand, paced back and forth, drawing a straight line across the wooden floor, his heels creating a rhythmic clicking sound.

"We must approach this tactfully, Thomas," Edward said, taking a small bottle of ink and starting to write a list of names. "These families have already been affected by the tragedy. We don't want to appear insensitive or intrusive."

Thomas nodded, stopping his gait and looking at Edward. "You are right, but we must also be direct. We have to find out if there is a hidden motive behind these deaths."

After a moment's reflection, Edward proposed: "Perhaps we could present ourselves as part of a medical investigation, trying to better understand the plague and its victims."

Thomas raised an eyebrow, "That's a brilliant idea. But how do we make sure they don't hide important details?"

"We will ask about their recent activities, travels, new encounters, anything that might give us a clue," Edward replied. "We have to be attentive and observe every little detail."

Silence crept between the two men as they both lost themselves in their own thoughts, pondering the possible ramifications of their investigation. Candlelight danced across Thomas's face, reflecting his growing emotion.

"Edward," Thomas began in a lower voice, "If there really is a murderer out there using the plague as a cover, we must stop him. This isn't just an investigation for justice, it could mean the safety of London."

Edward looked up, meeting Thomas's penetrating gaze. "I know, my friend. And we will not stop until we have answers."

The two men spent the next few hours drawing up a detailed plan. They decided to start by visiting the residence of Lord Harrington, one of London's most influential merchants and a recent victim. Edward had personally treated Lord Harrington shortly before his death and recalled that, despite the typical symptoms of the plague, something was amiss.

"My cousin used to work for Lord Harrington," Thomas said, "He told me he had recently made a trip to the continent and met several influential people. Maybe some of them know something." Edward noted this information, "A good place to start. We will visit his family tomorrow morning."

As the rain continued to fall, the two men finished organising their plan of action. Thomas stood up and walked to the door, "Get some rest, Edward. Tomorrow will be a long day."

Edward nodded, "And you be careful. If what we suspect is true, we could be in danger."

Thomas gave a reassuring smile, "Fear not. We are on the same team and we protect each other."

With these reassuring words, Thomas went out into the rainy night, leaving Edward alone with his thoughts and the slowly burning candles.

The Harrington Family

The Harrington mansion stood imposingly in a quiet London alley, separated from the chaos of the city by its high wrought-iron fence and lush garden. The arched windows and ivy-covered walls conveyed an aura of prestige and antiquity.

Thomas and Edward stopped in front of the large carved wooden gate, hesitating for a moment before knocking. Thomas glanced at Edward, "Remember, we are trying to help them. We don't want them to think we suspect them."

Edward nodded, "We need their information, not their hostility."

After a brief moment, a young maid opened the door. "May I help you, gentlemen?" she asked in a shy voice.

"We are here to talk about Lord Harrington's recent passing," Edward replied, showing a letter of introduction.

The maid showed them into an elegant drawing room. Mahogany furniture, rich carpets and family portraits adorned the room. "Wait a moment, I will inform Lady of your presence," said the maid, disappearing into an adjacent door.

While they waited, Thomas approached a portrait of Lord Harrington. The man portrayed had a piercing gaze and an expression of authority. 'I wonder what really happened to this man,' he whispered.

Shortly after, Lady Harrington and her daughter, Lady Amelia, entered. Lady Harrington, dressed in black as a sign of mourning, had delicate but severe features, while Amelia, with her golden hair and blue eyes, exuded a fresh beauty.

"Good morning, gentlemen," Lady Harrington began, "I'm told you want to talk about my husband's death. Although it is painful, if you think you can help..."

Edward nodded, "We are here to try to better understand the circumstances of his death. Any information would be helpful."

Amelia took the floor, "Shortly before his death, my father received some letters... he didn't want me to know, but I saw them. They were threatening."

Edward and Thomas' eyes met. This was a clue they were looking for. "Could we see these letters?" asked Thomas.

Amelia nodded and stood up, going to another room. When she returned, she held a small stack of letters in her hands. 'Here,' she said, handing them to Edward.

As he scrolled through the letters, Edward felt a chill run down his spine. They were written in irregular, almost feverish handwriting, and contained veiled threats and accusations against Lord Harrington. "These... these could be the proof we've been looking for," he said slowly.

Lady Harrington, with an expression of growing distress, asked: "Do you mean to say that my husband might have been murdered?"

Thomas replied gently, "It is too early to say, but there are some inconsistencies in the recent deaths we are examining."

Edward intervened, "Please keep this information confidential. We do not want to cause panic or endanger other people."

Amelia, with a trembling voice, said, "We will help you in any way we can. My father did not deserve such an end."

With a nod of thanks, Thomas and Edward took their leave, leaving behind a distraught but determined family to find the truth.

THE BROTHERHOOD OF THE PLAGUE

The Trap

Edward was in low spirits, frustrated to see his theory of suspicious deaths proving more and more likely and correct, but at the same time he could not extract any details, signs or clues that could lead to the murderer.

With this conviction he thought of daring an unpredictable and risky move, a plan that exposed him to danger and made him a decoy to bring out the killer.

Convinced of this gamble, he wanted to tell Thomas about it during a convivial meeting in an anonymous and discreet tavern.

Dusk light tinged the rooftops of London, and the air was pervaded by a heavy atmosphere. In a dimly lit tavern, Edward and Thomas sat at a secluded table, discussing the plan. The flickering candlelight reflected the conflict in Thomas's eyes.

The tavern was located in a narrow cobbled street, surrounded by multi-storey wooden buildings. Outside, the hanging sign swung in the wind, depicting a rampant lion and a pint of beer. The entrance featured a sturdy wooden door, with small, rounded windows covered by thick, distorted glass.

Inside, the atmosphere was warm and cosy. The floor was made of sturdy, creaking wooden planks. A large, crackling flame burned in the fireplace, illuminating the room and warming the many patrons seated around rustic wooden tables. The men, dressed in period clothing, wore waistcoats, long trousers and wide-brimmed hats, while the women wore long dresses and colourful shawls. The voices of people chatting, laughing and singing could be heard, while the smell of cooked food wafted through the air.

On the walls, old tapestries and hanging weapons tell stories of times gone by. A bartender in a dirty apron serves beer and ale from large wooden barrels, while a woman with a basket of hot breads goes from table to table. In one corner, a small stage houses a musician playing a lute, entertaining guests.

In this environment, the two confronted each other. "Edward, are you sure about this?" asked Thomas, his voice low but intense. "It's dangerous. That assassin has struck too many times already."

Edward looked at his friend, his expression resolute. "I know, Thomas, but if there's a chance to draw him out and stop him, we have to try. And given my involvement, I'm the obvious choice."

Thomas hesitated, then sighed, "You are stubborn, you know that? But if that's how it has to be, at least let me help you plan it."

The two men focused on the details. Edward would be visible, frequenting crowded places, flaunting his research into the killer and spreading the word that he had discovered something crucial. The goal was to attract the killer's attention and induce him to take the next step.

THE BROTHERHOOD OF THE PLAGUE

"Let's meet here every night," Thomas suggested. "If you notice anything strange or suspect you are being followed, let me know immediately."

"I will," Edward promised, "and Thomas, if anything should happen to me..."

Thomas interrupted him, laying a hand on his friend's shoulder. "Don't talk about it. I won't let anything happen to you."

The following week was tense. Edward followed the plan to the letter, making himself very visible and openly discussing his work. Every evening, he returned to the tavern and reported to Thomas what he had observed. So far, no sign of the killer.

One evening, as Edward was returning home from a conference, he heard faint footsteps behind him. He increased his pace, trying not to show fear, but the footsteps continued to follow him. He could see a hooded figure in the half-light. His heart beat wildly as he tried to remember the path to the tavern.

Finally, he glimpsed the light of the tavern in the distance. But just when he thought he was safe, a cold hand grabbed him in the shoulder. Edward turned, finding himself face to face with the hooded man. Before he could scream, a familiar voice rang through the air, "Let him go!"

Thomas emerged from the shadows, his gun pointed at his assailant. The hooded man, surprised, let go of Edward and fled. Edward, panting, looked gratefully at Thomas.

"I told you I would watch over you," Thomas said, smiling slightly.

Edward smiled in turn, "Thank you, my friend."

The two men knew that the danger had not yet passed, but now they were certain that the murderer knew about them. And that would bring them one step closer to unmasking him.

"We must insist, continue to tease him and wait for him to make a mistake." So spoke Edward in front of the puzzled face of Thomas who, at the end of a long and tortuous silence, agreed to continue this plan, guaranteeing his discreet presence to protect him.

The streets of London, typically bustling and full of life, now had a darker atmosphere. A thin layer of fog enveloped the buildings and streets, creating an aura of mystery and secrecy. Lanterns hanging from lampposts diffused a faint light, casting twisted shadows on the pavement.

Edward walked briskly, his black coat billowing behind him. Every now and then he would stop to converse with passers-by or enter some tavern. In each conversation, he clearly mentioned his interest in mysterious deaths and the strange carvings behind the ears of victims. His voice was firm and confident, but those who knew him would notice a tension in his eyes, a shadow of worry.

While Edward made his rounds, Thomas followed him from afar, keeping a certain distance so as not to arouse suspicion.

Hidden in alleys and behind the angles of buildings, he kept an eye on every movement, ready to intervene at the first sign of danger.

In one of the breaks, as Edward entered a tavern, Thomas hid behind a stack of wooden crates. He pulled a small flask of whisky from his pocket and took a sip, trying to calm his nerves. "This is crazy," he muttered to himself. "Where is that assassin? He can't have changed his plans now that he knows Edward is on his trail."

Inside the tavern, Edward sat at the bar, ordering a glass of beer. A man sitting next to him, with a thick red beard and a curious air, looked at him with interest.

"Listen, are you that doctor who investigates mysterious deaths?" the man asked.

Edward nodded, keeping his guard up. "Yes, it's me. Why?"

The man lowered his voice, looking around as if afraid of being overheard. "I hear there's someone who doesn't want you to dig too much.... You must be careful."

Edward stared at him intensely. "Who told you this?"

But before the man could answer, a dull noise from the street attracted everyone's attention. Edward jumped up and ran outside, followed by Thomas who had suddenly appeared.

Outside, a wagon had overturned, and a small crowd had gathered around it. It looked like an accident, but Edward and

Thomas knew it could be a diversion. They looked into each other's eyes, the understanding muted between them.

"I must continue," Edward said with determination. "If the killer is here, I want him to know that I will not give up."

Thomas nodded, "And I will be with you every step of the way." The rest of the night passed without further incident. But the stakeout had revealed one thing: the killer was aware of their presence and was playing a dangerous game. It was a hunt, and Edward and Thomas were now the hunters.

The first light of dawn flooded the room through the thick velvet curtains, faintly reflecting off the wooden surfaces and the numerous stacked books. Edward, his hair a little dishevelled and his face marked by the night he had just spent, was sitting at his desk, surrounded by drawings, notes and reports. His obsession with the case had completely absorbed him.

When Thomas entered, bringing with him the fresh aroma of the morning, Edward seemed lost in thought. But the attention of both of them was immediately caught by an envelope sealed with red sealing wax, placed in the centre of the desk.

"It was under the door when I arrived," said Thomas, with a tone of concern.

Edward took it with trembling hands, noting the absence of a sender. Carefully, he broke the seal and unfolded the paper inside. The writing was precise, almost artistic, but what the words revealed was disturbing.

THE BROTHERHOOD OF THE PLAGUE

"Dear Edward,

I am aware of your investigations and your attempts to hunt me down. I admire your determination, but I advise you to stop. You already know too much, and I'd hate to have to add a talented man like you to my list.

You can consider this a friendly warning. I'm not an enemy unless you want me to be. The choice is yours. But know that I am watching you, ever more closely.

With esteem,

Your not-so-secret admirer.

A heavy silence enveloped the room. Edward slowly reread the letter, trying to assimilate every word. Thomas moved closer, also reading the contents over his friend's shoulder.

"Edward, we have to take these threats seriously," Thomas said with unusual gravity.

Edward ran a hand through his hair, trying to keep calm. 'I know. But who could want me dead? And why? I'm just a doctor."

Thomas leaned over the desk, bringing his face closer to Edward's. "My friend, you are not 'just' a doctor. You are the only one who has connected these deaths and is getting closer to the truth. This could endanger many influential people."

Edward sighed heavily, "So what should we do?"

Thomas seemed to reflect for a moment. 'First of all, we have to step up our security measures. Next, we need to try to find out who might have reason to want you out of the picture. Someone you've met recently? Someone who might have information on the killer?"

Edward reflected, thinking back over the previous days. "I don't know, Thomas. But one thing is certain: we can't give up now. We have to find this killer and put him behind bars. Before he hurts more people. There's a list, so he wrote, other victims."

Thomas nodded, determined. "You are right. And together, we will make it."

The revelation of the letter had changed everything. But instead of frightening them, it had only strengthened their determination to solve the mystery. Both knew the danger was real, but they were ready to face it, at each other's side.

The discovery

Gossip

Dusk had enveloped the city in a blanket of shadow. Street lamps spread a flickering yellow light in the cobblestone streets, and the air was laden with the smell of burnt wood and spices.

Edward and Thomas had taken refuge in a tavern called 'The Dancing Rat'. The structure had thick stone walls and a low ceiling. Large wooden barrels were stacked along one wall, while rough wooden tables were occupied by men and women relaxing after a long day's work. The chatter of patrons, laughter and the songs of a bard filled the air.

Thomas nodded to a man sitting alone in a corner. His hair was tousled, his beard unkempt, and his clothes were dirty and threadbare. He held a bottle of liquor tightly in his hands, and occasionally cast shifty glances at the other customers.

"Look there," said Thomas, "that old Jeb is completely tipsy tonight. They say when he drinks too much, he starts telling stories of things seen and heard."

Edward observed the man for a moment. "Do you think he might know something?"

Thomas shrugged his shoulders. "You never know. Drunks have a habit of revealing secrets."

Determined to find out more and with nothing to lose, they approached Jeb's table. Edward took a chair and sat down opposite the man. "Good evening, Jeb," he began in a friendly tone. "Looks like you've had a long day."

Jeb lifted his gaze, his bloodshot eyes scrutinised Edward for a moment before returning to the bottle. "Who are you to judge?" he murmured.

Edward smiled. "None, my friend. We are only interested in your stories."

Jeb laughed, a hoarse, bitter sound. "Stories? Oh, I have many. But the most disturbing one is about a group of powerful people who meet at night. They say they are responsible for many dark things that happen in the city."

Thomas leaned forward. "Who are you talking about?"

The old man paused, sipping from the bottle. "The Brotherhood of the Plague," he whispered, glancing around as if afraid of being overheard.

Edward and Thomas exchanged a glance. "What do you know about them?" asked Edward.

Jeb leaned back, a cunning smile on his lips. 'They say they control everything, from who lives to who dies. That the plague is not just a disease, but a means to exert their power. And that those who oppose them disappear into thin air."

Thomas and Edward remained silent, absorbing the man's words. It was a lead, and even if it came from a drunk in a tavern, it was a start.

"Thank you, Jeb," Edward said, getting up. He left some coins on the table as thanks. "Have another glass."

As they left the tavern, the cold air hit them like a fist. "What do you think?" asked Thomas.

Edward looked up at the moon shining in the sky. "I think we are on the right track. And that this investigation could be much bigger than we thought."

And with that information, the two continued their mission, determined to discover the truth about this Brotherhood of the Plague.

The following day, as the sun's rays filtered through the thick clouds of a gloomy morning, Edward and Thomas found themselves at a flea market. The place was a maze of stalls, tents and stalls, with merchants of all kinds offering their wares, from exotic spices to glittering jewellery.

THE BROTHERHOOD OF THE PLAGUE

Every place, especially these types of places could be a hotbed of information and Edward did not want to leave anything out in the search for clues, especially now, after this obscure Brotherhood of the Plague had materialised on the horizon.

Moreover, the plague was still raging in the city, continuing to claim victims and forcing everyone to take countless precautions.

As a doctor, he was aware that a place like that was ideal for transmitting the plague, but for the people it was one of the few opportunities to buy some goods cheaply, while for him it was a chance to gather some useful information.

Edward, with watchful eyes, was looking for something that might reveal more about the Brotherhood of the Plague. It was then, at a stall selling antique coins and medallions, that his eyes were caught by a particular coin. It was bronze, with a greenish patina caused by time. But what struck him was the image engraved on one side: a black rat with angel wings.

"Here's something interesting," Edward said, taking the coin and showing it to Thomas.

Thomas observed her carefully. "A rat with angel wings? What the hell does that mean?"

The merchant, an old man with a grey beard and thick glasses, stepped forward. "Ah, I see you have found my most unusual coin. It is rare, very rare. And, of course, very expensive."

THE BROTHERHOOD OF THE PLAGUE

Edward looked at him. "Where does it come from? And what does it represent?"

The merchant leaned over the counter, his eyes scanning Edward. 'Well, you should know, that coin is said to have belonged to a member of the Brotherhood of the Plague. The rat represents the plague, of course. But the angel wings . Well, they are said to symbolise purification through death."

Edward and Thomas exchanged a glance. They had found something concrete. "How much do you want for this coin?" asked Thomas.

The merchant smiled. "For you, fifty gold coins."

Thomas grimaced. "It is overpriced."

'History has a price, young man,' replied the merchant.

Edward, without hesitation, placed the fifty gold coins on the counter. "We'll take it," he said. He had a feeling that that coin might be useful to him.

With the coin safely in their pockets, the two walked away from the market. "What are you going to do now?" asked Thomas.

Edward pulled out the coin and looked at it in the sunlight. "This symbol means something. We must find out where to find the Brotherhood and perhaps where they meet and what they intend to do. And this coin could be our guide."

Thomas nodded, convinced. "Then let's go and find out the truth, whatever it is although I don't see how this coin will help us."

As they walked through the cobbled streets, the coin seemed to weigh much more than it should, as if it carried with it the weight of dark and sinister secrets waiting to be revealed. And both were curious to discover what lay behind the winged rat symbol.

In a quiet side street, far from the buzz of the central market, was a small bookshop called 'The Secret of the Pages'. The façade was worn by time, the windows covered with a thick layer of dust that prevented passers-by from peeking inside. The bell on the door jingled melodiously as Edward and Thomas entered.

The interior was a labyrinth of shelves packed with books, maps and scrolls of parchment. The air was thick with the scent of old paper and leather. Behind a wooden desk, an elderly bookseller with a pair of magnifying glasses hanging from his neck was examining a manuscript.

"Can I help you?" he asked, looking up at the two.

"We are looking for information on a sect called 'The Brotherhood of the Plague'," Edward replied, showing the coin with the winged rat.

The bookseller's face contorted into a grimace of concern. "That is ancient history, dear sir. Not many people talk about it openly."

Edward approached the bench. "We have reasons to believe that this cult is still active and causing a lot of pain in the city. Any information you could share would be of great help."

The bookseller looked at the coin and then back at Edward. "I see you are serious about this." He sighed and pointed to a hidden shelf in a dark corner of the bookshop. "Perhaps what you seek can be found there."

Edward and Thomas walked over to the indicated shelf and started leafing through the volumes. After a few minutes, Edward pulled out a black leather-bound book with a faded title: 'Secrets of the Brotherhood'.

Carefully opening the book, he discovered that it was a diary of a Brotherhood member dating back to the last century. The pages contained details of how the group had been founded with the aim of 'purifying' the city through the sacrifice of individuals deemed impure. There were also references to secret rituals and ceremonies.

"Thomas, look at this!" exclaimed Edward, showing him a particularly interesting page. It was a map of the city, with several points marked with the winged rat symbol.

"These must be the places where they gathered, but then it really exists, it's not a popular invention or the result of an old drunkard's delusions," said Thomas, examining the map.

The bookseller, approaching, intervened: "If you intend to investigate these places, be careful. The Brotherhood is powerful and has allies in high places. They are not to be underestimated."

Edward nodded. "Thank you for your help. How much do we owe for the book?"

The bookseller smiled faintly. "Consider it a gift. I hope it can help you, may God protect you."

Thomas looked at Edward, his face tense. 'We have to be careful, Edward. This is not a treasure hunt. These people are dangerous."

Edward, clutching the book to his chest, replied, "I know. But we have to do the right thing, do you want me to let such dangerous people run around the city?."

As they left the library, the cold evening air enveloped them. But now they had an extra weapon: knowledge. And with that book in hand, they were one step ahead in their search for the Brotherhood of the Plague.

Infiltration

The old warehouse located on the edge of town was, at first glance, an abandoned building, but Edward and Thomas had spent days monitoring the spots mapped in the book and eventually noticed a steady stream of people, all dressed in dark hoods to conceal their identities, entering the warehouse during the night hours.

Hidden behind barrels in the nearby alley, the two watched every movement. The sky was leaden, and a light rain fell silently, making the atmosphere even more tense.

"Look there," whispered Thomas, pointing to a burly man with a thick, grey beard who seemed to be guarding the entrance. "That could be a problem."

Edward nodded, pulled out a small pair of binoculars from his bag and used it to peer inside through a broken window. "I see at least a dozen people inside, and they are all wearing the same black hood with the winged rat symbol."

Thomas chewed his lip. "Well, we've scouted them. How do you intend to approach them?"

Edward paused, reflecting. "We need to divide their attention. You create a distraction at the entrance while I sneak in from behind."

With a nod of agreement, the two put their plan into action. Thomas approached the warehouse, deliberately tripping over the barrels, making a noise loud enough to attract the guard's attention.

"Who goes there?" shouted the man, running towards Thomas.

Taking advantage of the distraction, Edward quickly made his way to the back of the building, finding a small door ajar. He sneaked in and hid behind some crates. The interior of the warehouse was lit by candles. A large circle had been drawn on the floor and, in its centre, an altar on which lay a large open book and various ritual instruments.

Inside the circle, members of the Brotherhood were chanting monotonous songs. Edward recognised some of them: they were nobles and prominent citizens of the city. He then understood the depth and influence of this sect.

The floor of the great hall was covered with large dark red velvet carpets, which muffled every step and sound. Huge silver candelabra, filled with black candles, cast a flickering shadow on the walls decorated with strange pagan symbols and images of monstrous-looking creatures.

In the centre of the hall was a large black stone altar, above which hung a large oval mirror, framed in gold and silver. It was clear that the mirror had some ritual significance, as in front of it stood a masked figure, dressed in silver and black priestly robes, reciting formulae in an ancient and forgotten language.

Edward, hidden behind an archway, tried to understand the meaning of what he was observing. He saw members of the Brotherhood, masked in gold and silver masks depicting animals and mythological creatures, form a circle around the altar. Each of them held a small ceremonial dagger, its handle inlaid with precious stones.

THE BROTHERHOOD OF THE PLAGUE

The figure in the centre began to chant in a deep, hypnotic voice: 'O Ancient Gods, hear our cry! The plague advances and asks for your protection. We offer sacrifice in your name, that your wrath may subside and the city be spared!"

One of the members approached the altar carrying a small animal, probably a rat, and placed it on top. With a swift and confident gesture, the central figure used the dagger to sacrifice the animal, allowing its blood to drip onto the altar and then fall into a small golden bowl.

"By the gods of plague and death, accept this sacrifice and spare our people!" exclaimed the figure, as the other members repeated the formula in a monotonous chorus.

Edward felt a chill run down his spine. It was clear that the Brotherhood believed strongly in their cause, to the point of performing ritual sacrifices in honour of the ancients.

As the ritual continued, Edward noticed a detail that made him shudder. On a side table, he saw several small wax figures, each representing a person, and noticed that some of them had a small incision behind the ear, just like the victims he had studied.

Edward, with measured, careful and slow movements moved towards a side room.

The room was a cross between a library and a shrine, with tall dark oak shelves filled with ancient manuscripts and dusty tomes. A large mahogany desk stood in the centre, lit by the dim light of an oil lamp. Edward stealthily approached the desk, looking for something of value. He knew that every second counted, but he had to take advantage of the opportunity.

Suddenly, his gaze fell on a heavy leather-bound volume with a silver seal: the winged rat, symbol of the Brotherhood. He cautiously opened the book and found within it a series of finely written names, followed by dates and notations.

Next to many of the names, there was a sign: a cross. Edward felt a knot in his throat when he recognised some of those names. They were people he knew, some of them had already been found dead, with the same incision behind the ear.

Quickly, he tore the page out of the book and carefully folded it, slipping it into the inside pocket of his jacket. As he turned to leave the room, a firm voice stopped him in his tracks. "You were looking for this, I suppose," said a tall, slender figure wrapped in a dark cloak, mask on his face. His voice was as cold as ice.

Edward swallowed hard, trying to mask his nervousness. "Who are you? And what do you want from me?"

"The questions are irrelevant," the man replied, advancing towards Edward. "You have taken something that does not belong to you."

"It is you who are hurting innocent people," Edward retorted, trying to buy time.

The man laughed, a ghostly sound echoing through the room. "Innocent? No one is truly innocent. And those people were destined to die for a higher cause."

Edward thought quickly. "What if I give you what you want? What if I gave you the list back? We could strike a deal."

The figure seemed to ponder the proposal for a moment, but then said with contempt: "You cannot negotiate with fate, Edward. And now, it is your turn."

Edward prepared to face his opponent, but before he could move, an arrow hissed through the air, striking the masked figure in the chest. The man fell backwards, and out of the darkness Thomas appeared, bow still in hand.

"Sorry for the delay," Thomas said, helping Edward to his feet. "But I thought you might need a hand."

Edward smiled, still shaken by the experience. "Thank you, Thomas. I don't know what I would have done without you."

The two men quickly headed for the exit, knowing they would have little time before other members of the Brotherhood discovered them. But now they had concrete proof, a list of names that could help them stop the Brotherhood and their dark plans.

THE BROTHERHOOD OF THE PLAGUE

The list

Hurriedly returning to Edward's lab, the two sat down to take a breath and rethink what they had seen and how dangerous it had been.

By the flickering candlelight in Edward's workshop, the list of names they had stolen exuded a sinister aura. Thomas spread the sheet of paper on the table, staring at it with incredulous eyes. Each name was a life, a destiny. But one name in particular caught his attention, making him lose his breath: Edward Baines.

"Edward," Thomas began in a trembling voice, "your name is on the list."

Edward, who had been absorbed in thought, looked up at the list and his face suddenly paled. His trembling hand moved to his name written in black ink. He felt his heart pounding in his chest. "I wondered when they would decide that I had become too big a problem for them," he sighed.

Thomas jumped up, grabbing Edward by the shoulders. "We cannot take this situation lightly, Edward. This changes everything."

"I know," Edward replied, trying to regain his composure. "But we cannot allow this discovery to paralyse us with fear. We must act."

The room was shrouded in a tense silence, broken only by the crackling of candles and the ticking of the clock. Thomas began pacing back and forth, his face hollowed with worry. "How could they have known about your involvement? How could they have put your name on the list?"

Edward ran a hand through his hair. "Maybe through the people we interviewed or someone who saw us while we were investigating. Either way, we can't help but feel watched now."

The thought that someone might be aware of their moves was frightening. Edward stood up, walking over to a small chest of drawers near the window. "When I was a child," he began, "my grandfather used to tell me about the dark days, the moments when all seemed lost. He used to say that in those moments we had to find the light within ourselves." He opened a drawer and pulled out a small dagger with an inlaid handle. "This was my grandfather's. He used it to protect our family. Now it is our turn to protect what is dear to us."

Thomas looked at the shining blade, reflecting on the gravity of the situation. "We must protect you, Edward. Perhaps you should go somewhere safe, away from here."

Edward shook his head. "If I run away, they will have won. I will not allow that to happen."

Thomas sighed, knowing that he could not convince his friend to change his mind. "Then we must be ready," he said. "Every step, every decision could be fatal."

Edward nodded, "You are right. But we cannot afford to be afraid. The truth is on our side and we must use every means at our disposal to defeat this evil cult."

THE BROTHERHOOD OF THE PLAGUE

The meeting

Elize's advice

As Edward and Thomas argued, Elize came in to bring hot tea and as she poured it, still steaming, into cups, in an almost didactic tone she asked: "you keep groping in the dark and you don't know who you're really dealing with."

The two looked at each other dumbfounded and Thomas intervened, 'well, it seems normal to me, otherwise we would probably have already come to some conclusions.'

Edward also intervened, 'sorry Elize, but perhaps you have some advice to give us on this matter'. Remaining with a very detached tone and posture as if he did not want to give himself much importance or give the feeling that he had solutions at hand, Elize retorted "you are saying that this brotherhood wants to eliminate nobles, wealthy and influential merchants, if this is true I think it would be useful to confront someone of that rank, perhaps among them are even more aware of the risk they are taking and could even give you some useful pointers on the matter".

"sensible words ..." Edward intervened, "but people of that rank I knew are dead and one must be careful not to spread panic ... it's easy to spread panic, especially these days" Thomas nodded.

Elize, however, was unperturbed and said very calmly, 'if you wish, I know the Count of Montegue and I could organise a meeting for you, naturally not in his house, but in a discreet, anonymous place ... certain things must be dealt with away from one's own walls, especially in certain mansions where even the walls have ears and trust is not among the virtues most practised among certain people.

The two astonished men accepted the advice and gave their approval for Elize to organise this meeting.

Edward and Thomas walked side by side through narrow streets with little traffic, their shadows mingling with those of the torches hanging on the walls of the houses. Edward wore a long black coat with a high collar. Thomas, on the other hand, wore a brown waistcoat over a white shirt, with black trousers and high boots.

"Elize told us to look for a nobleman in this area," Edward said, looking around. "But how will we recognise him?"

Thomas laughed. "I guess a nobleman won't go unnoticed in a place like this."

While the two were conversing, a female figure appeared from an alley. She was Elize, wearing a blue dress with gold embroidery and carrying a fan in her hand.

"I was looking for you," he said with a smile. "The nobleman I mentioned is in that tavern, please be discreet," he pointed to a nearby building with a large wooden sign.

They entered the tavern, where the air was thick with smoke and the smell of beer and food filled the room. Seated at a table at the far end of the room, a man in fine clothes watched them. He had grey hair, a hollow face and intense blue eyes. He wore a blue silk suit with gold buttons and a ring with a crest on his finger.

Edward and Thomas approached cautiously, and the man greeted them with a nod. "Are you the ones who wanted to speak to me?"

"Yes," Edward replied. "Elize told us you might have some information on the Brotherhood of the Plague."

The man smiled slightly. " without preamble eh! Elize had told me ... I am the Earl of Montague. And yes! I have heard of that fraternity. But why do you care?"

Thomas intervened: "we suspect, something more, that the fraternity is active and that they are behind several suspicious deaths that have nothing to do with the plague, so we are looking for someone who either belongs to them or knows them and helps us to break them up before more deaths occur.

The Earl of Montague paused, sipping his wine. "Baron de Lacroix is an influential member of the Brotherhood," he finally said. "But I warn you, trying to interfere with their affairs can be dangerous."

Edward looked at Thomas, then back at the Count. "We have our reasons for seeking information. Can we count on your discretion?"

The Count nodded, 'Of course. But I advise you to be careful. The Brotherhood is not to be taken lightly."

As they left the tavern, the air had become colder. The shadows seemed even darker, and the hissing of the wind presaged the arrival of a storm.

"What are we going to do now?" asked Thomas.

Edward looked at the horizon. "We must find Baron de Lacroix. And find out what the Brotherhood of the Plague is plotting."

Comparison

It did not take long for Thomas, who had several contacts with the city guards, to locate the Baron's residence and there. Edward and Thomas headed there without delay. The residence of Baron de Lacroix, regarded and described as one of the high-ranking members of the Brotherhood, was imposing, situated on a hill overlooking the city. Its stone walls, illuminated by the dim light of dusk, exuded an aura of power and mystery. As they approached, Edward and Thomas could sense the tension in the air. They looked at each other, reinforcing their commitment to get answers.

After knocking firmly, they were greeted by a butler in a formal suit. "The Baron awaits you," he said in a cold and distant voice, amidst the surprised and astonished looks of the two visitors, leading them into a large and sumptuous hall. In the centre of the room, near a large, lit fireplace, Baron de Lacroix awaited them, seated in a red velvet armchair.

The Baron, a middle-aged man with silver hair and a well-groomed beard, stared at the two visitors with piercing eyes. "Ah, Edward and Thomas," he said in a calm but authoritative voice. "I have heard of your little investigations. What can I do for you this evening?"

Edward caught his breath, trying to control his agitation. 'We want answers, Baron. We know about your involvement with the Brotherhood of the Plague. We want to know more and why."

The Baron laughed, a deep, resounding sound echoing through the room. "Your accusations are very serious. But I admire your courage. I wonder, though, if you are really ready to hear the truth."

Thomas stepped forward, his face tense. "We came here for the truth. And we are ready for anything to get it."

The Baron crossed his hands on his lap, tilting his head slightly. 'The Brotherhood of the Plague has existed for centuries, even before your ancestors were born. We firmly believe that the plague is a divine punishment, a punishment for sinful humanity. In this context there are people on a list, called the 'appointed', they are individuals chosen to appease the fury of the gods, through their sacrifices."

Edward became agitated, anger and dismay visible on his face. "So you kill innocent people in the name of the gods? How can you justify such horror?"

The Baron looked at him intensely. 'It is not a question of justification. It is a matter of faith. We believe that, through these sacrifices, we can save humanity from total ruin. And if that means we have to do hard deeds, we will do it without hesitation."

Thomas shook his head. 'This is absurd. You cannot play gods. You cannot decide who lives and who dies."

The Baron stood up slowly, approaching the two men. "Look around you, Thomas. The plague has ravaged this city. People we love have died. The Brotherhood is simply trying to find a solution, to find a way out of this darkness."

Edward, trying to control his anger, replied: "Killing innocent people is not a solution. It is a crime."

The Baron smiled sadly. "Sometimes, the end justifies the means. And, in any case, did you really think you could stop a Brotherhood that has endured for centuries?"

With those words, the Baron gestured to the butler, who promptly rang a bell. A few moments later, the door opened, and several strong men entered the hall, closing the door behind them.

Edward and Thomas realised the danger they were in, they looked around to see if there was a way out, but it was too late to escape, the number of men in the room was overwhelming.

Baron de Lacroix looked at the two men with a mixture of sorrow and determination. "I would have preferred it had not come to this," he sighed. "But I cannot allow you to interfere with the work of the Brotherhood." With a nod, he gave the order for his men to take Edward and Thomas.

Prisoners of the Baron

The moment the Baron's men grabbed Edward and Thomas, a feeling of panic and shock invaded them. Both were writhing, trying to free themselves, but the grip was too strong. Quick as lightning, they were bound with thick ropes and their faces were hooded, obliterating all perception of light.

Thomas tried to speak, but the words came out choked by the heavy fabric of the hood. He could hear Edward's laboured breathing next to him, he knew his friend was also struggling with growing fear.

"Damn them!" shouted Edward, the anger palpable in his voice. But his challenge was met only by the dull sound of footsteps and the creaking of wagons in the distance.

On the way, smells and sounds became the only clues to their environment. They perceived the strong scent of hay, the sound of a market, the murmur of voices. But with their hands tied and their eyes blindfolded, their world became dark and disorienting.

The journey seemed interminable. The two were forced to walk for what seemed like hours, pulled by unknown forces. The road beneath their feet changed from cobblestones to dirt, suggesting that they were moving away from the city.

Finally, they heard a heavy wooden door open, followed by the rumble of footsteps in an echoing room. The air was cold and damp, the smell of mould and rot hit them strongly. Without warning, they were thrown to the floor, the ropes that bound them were loosened and their headphones removed.

Emerging into the darkness, their eyes took a moment to adjust. They were in an underground prison. The walls were made of rough stones and the floor was a mixture of earth and stones. In the centre of the cell, an iron bar protruded from the floor, to which other victims, clearly long-time prisoners, were chained.

Thomas looked around, searching for a way out, but the heavy iron bars on the windows and the solid wooden door suggested that there was no way out. Edward, sitting next to him, had eyes full of anger and determination.

"They can't keep us here," he hissed. "We have to find a way out."

Thomas nodded, "I agree. But first, we need to understand where we are and what they want from us."

As they tried to process their situation, one of the Baron's men entered the cell, a mocking smile on his lips. "The Baron will send for you when he is ready," he said in a tone of superiority. "In the meantime, I suggest you enjoy your new home."

Edward stood up, his gaze fixed on the man. 'It will not end like this,' he promised firmly.

The man laughed. "That's what they all say." And with that mocking reply, he walked away, leaving Edward and Thomas in the darkness, desperately searching for a way out of their captivity.

Despite the cold humidity and the terror of the situation, the underground cell was animated by a soft murmur of voices. Several people, chained like Edward and Thomas, were scattered around the room. Some were silent, their shoulders hunched, while others spoke softly to their neighbours.

As Edward and Thomas adjusted to their new reality, a grey-bearded old man sat next to them and watched them with scrutinising eyes.

"Newcomers, eh?" he said in a rough voice. "I am Geoffrey. I've been here for months, maybe years. I've lost count."

Thomas looked at him, trying to hide his anxiety. "Why are you here, Geoffrey?"

The old man laughed bitterly. 'For daring to defy the Baron, of course. I tried to protect my village from his men and his exorbitant taxes. But as you see, it did not work."

A few steps away from them, a young woman with dull eyes stared at the floor. "I am Clara," she said in a trembling voice. "I was caught trying to escape the city with my son. I don't know where they took him."

Edward, feeling helpless, placed a reassuring hand on the woman's shoulder. "We are sorry, Clara. We will do our best to help you."

Further into the cell, a muscular man with scars on his arms and face spoke aloud. "I am Rowan," he said, pointing to the scars. "I have been a fighter all my life. But even I could not stand against the Baron and his men. I fought to protect my family, but they... they were stronger."

Thomas nodded, respecting the man's courage. "We need to unite and find a way out," he suggested.

Another prisoner, a young man with a thick black beard, intervened. "I am Cedric. There were seven of us brothers. Now I am the only one left. The others were all killed for daring to challenge the Baron."

As the stories were told, a common theme became clear: the Baron was a tyrant, and these people had been imprisoned for daring to oppose him.

Edward, feeling inspired by the stories of endurance and courage, stood up. "We have to find a way out of here," he said with determination. "We cannot allow our stories to end here, in this cell."

The other prisoners nodded in agreement or resigned hope, but it was clear from their faces and looks that it was impossible to leave that place.

Betrayal

Time in the prison passed slowly. Each hour was an exhausting wait, an extension of the suffering Edward and Thomas were forced to endure. Their bodies were weak and hungry, but their spirits refused to fade, clinging to the fragile thread of hope.

THE BROTHERHOOD OF THE PLAGUE

The air was stale and putrid. The stone walls were damp to the touch, exuding the dampness of the subsoil. The poor lighting, provided by smoky torches, created shadows that seemed to stretch ominously. Edward and Thomas were forced to lie on uncomfortable, vermin-infested straw cots.

One morning, awoken by heavy footsteps and metallic clanging, they struggled to get up. A few armoured guards in brass armour made their way through the rows of prisoners, their swords clinking as they moved. At the end of the procession, there was an imposing figure dressed in rich robes: The Baron. Next to him was a woman wrapped in a black cloak, whose figure was familiar to Edward.

As they approached, Edward recognised the figure: it was Elize. Edward's eyes filled with dismay and anger. She, the confidante on whom he had placed his trust, now walked beside their enemy.

"Elize?" whispered Thomas in a voice broken with astonishment. "How could you?"

The Baron, noticing the reaction of the two men, laughed under his breath. 'Oh, I see you know each other. Splendid! Elize has been an excellent source of information about you."

Elize did not meet their gaze. She looked sad, but also resolute in her choice.

Edward, fighting back tears of anger and betrayal, found the strength to speak. "Why, Elize? Why did you betray us?"

She looked up, her green eyes shining with complex emotions. "I had no choice, Edward. The Baron threatened to kill my family if I did not cooperate."

The Baron put his hand on her shoulder, as if to claim his victory. "You see, everyone has a price. Even your dear Elize."

Thomas, trying to keep calm, said: 'You are a monster. Using people, threatening them.... You will not rest until we have our revenge."

The Baron smiled mischievously. "You have spirit, I must admit. But let's see how long it lasts."

Edward, trying to put aside his grief and anger, stared Elize in the eyes. "No matter what happens, know that I will never forgive you for this."

Elize looked at Edward, tears in her eyes. "I'm sorry, Edward," she whispered. "I'm really sorry."

But Elize's words were only a distant echo for Edward. His heart was broken, and the pain of betrayal was like a sharp blade cutting through his soul. The Baron and Elize's surprise visit had left a wound that would never heal. And as the guards drove them away, Edward and Thomas were determined to fight harder than ever for their survival, freedom and justice.

THE BROTHERHOOD OF THE PLAGUE

The City in the Grasp of the Plague

Meanwhile, the plague raged in the city, claiming victims and obscuring every thought of life. The struggle for survival became strenuous and at the same time futile, the disease showed no signs of letting up. The city streets, once bustling with laughter, conversation and trade, were now desolate and silent. The fear of the plague had turned the ancient city centre into a place of death and desolation. The houses were boarded up, with heavy wooden beams at the doors and red marks on the facades, symbolising the disease that had struck the inhabitants.

From time to time, rickety carts drawn by skinny horses drove along the streets, picking up the bodies of those who had fallen victim to the disease. "Bring out your dead!" shouted the man with the cart, his hoarse voice echoing mournfully in the silence. His words were followed by the weeping of the bereaved families.

"Mother, why did heaven punish us like this?" whispered a young woman, Alina, looking with red, swollen eyes at the motionless figure of her younger sister lying on a straw bed.

"I don't know, my dear," the mother replied, shaking her daughter's hand. "But we must have faith and hope for better times."

Churches, once places of worship and hope, had become makeshift hospitals. Priests, dressed in long robes and wearing beaked masks, tried to cure the sick with prayers and ancient remedies, often ineffective against the devastating power of the plague.

Father Matthew, an old priest with a grey beard, told one of his confreres: "We don't have enough food or medicine. And people are losing faith, I fear they will soon turn their backs on us."

The confrere, Father John, nodded sadly. "We must do what we can, Matthew. This is God's will and we must accept it."

In the heart of the city, the main square had been transformed into an immense bonfire. Great flames danced towards the sky, fed by the bodies of the dead, in the hope that the fire would purify the air and stop the spread of the disease. The acrid smell of smoke permeated every corner of the city, a constant reminder of the tragedy that was happening. At one corner of the square, a group of people had gathered around a man in a black hoodie. He was Dr Lorenz, a doctor who claimed to have a cure for the plague.

"Come, come!" he exclaimed. "I have found a cure! A potion that can save your lives!"

But his voice was drowned out by the wails of the sick and the cries of the families. People, now desperate, were willing to believe any hope, even if it seemed too good to be true.

In a narrow alley, two men argued furtively. "The plague is a punishment," one of them whispered, his eye grim and gaze fierce. "We must make a sacrifice to some god to appease this slaughter."

His companion nodded, his eyes full of fear. "Yes, we must do something, before it is too late."

As the plague continued to claim victims, despair grew. Trust in institutions and the church diminished, while rumours of plots and sacrifices grew. The once proud and flourishing city was now a place of death, fear and superstition. And in the midst of this darkness, men were ready for anything to find a way out.

THE BROTHERHOOD OF THE PLAGUE

The occasion

The plague arrives in prison

The prison was located on the edge of town, an old stone building with high walls and small, grated windows. The interior was damp and cold, with dark cells opening onto long narrow corridors. The plague, which had already devastated the city, also found fertile ground within the thick walls of the prison.

Sneezing and coughing became constant sounds, echoing through the corridors like premonitions of death. The prisoners, already weak and malnourished, became easy prey to the disease. Their cells became small tombs, and the number of those being taken away daily increased dramatically.

"Look! Antony has the plague too!" whispered George, a thin prisoner with an unkempt beard, pointing to a man in a nearby cell. Antony was lying on the floor, shivering, with dark spots on his skin.

"Madonna mia," murmured Marc, George's cellmate. "God help us. We don't stand a chance in here."

The guards, who once exercised their power over the internees with cruelty, now trembled with fear. Even they were not immune. Some of them had already shown symptoms, and their colleagues avoided them like the plague.

"I don't want to die in this hole!" exclaimed one of the guards, Paul, a burly man with a scar on his cheek. "We must do something!"

"What do you suggest?" asked Pieter, another guard, sarcastically, as he observed the prisoners through the bars. "We cannot escape. And if we did, the city would be no refuge. The plague is everywhere."

Inside the cells, despair grew. The prisoners began to pray, to cry, to scream. Some tried to comfort each other, while others resigned themselves to their fate.

"Somehow, maybe this is right," murmured Lorenz, an elderly prisoner with long white hair. "Perhaps this is God's punishment for our sins."

"Don't talk nonsense," retorted his cellmate, Rafael. "We are all victims, innocent or guilty. This disease makes no distinction."

Weeks passed, and the prison grew quieter and quieter. Death prowled through the cells, taking with it, one after the other. But despite the tragedy, small acts of humanity emerged from the shadows.

One day, one of the guards brought cool water to a feverish prisoner. "Drink," he said softly, supporting the man's head. "Perhaps it will help you."

The prisoner, his eyes shining, whispered, "Thank you." It was a small kindness, but at that moment it meant everything.

The cells, once filled with men, were now largely empty. The prison, which once echoed with the sounds of life, was now as silent as a tomb. But within the thick walls, hope was not completely lost. Those who survived the plague were slowly beginning to pick themselves up, to comfort each other, to rebuild their lives, piece by piece. The tragedy had shown the worst in humanity, but it had also revealed the best: love, compassion and resilience in the face of adversity.

A Glimmer of Hope

In the prison where the plague had now taken over, despair permeated every corner. Empty cells and inert bodies were now a common sight. But amidst the tragedy, a glimmer of hope made its way in.

As death took more and more victims, one of the guards began to show symptoms. His forehead was hot and sweaty, his face pale and his eyes bloodshot. He remembered hearing that Edward, one of the prisoners, was a doctor. Between fear and despair, she decided to seek his help.

"Damn, you look like a spectre," said Paul, the scarred guard, looking at his feverish colleague.

"Can't you feel it? This heat... these twinges...," he murmured in a trembling voice. "I think... I think I have the plague."

Paul swallowed hard. "We need help. I heard that prisoner, Edward, is a doctor."

They then decided to take a risk. They freed Edward from his cell, his hands still tied but free to move.

"Edward," Paul said in a strained voice, "you're a doctor, right? My partner is sick. Can you help him?"

Edward, surprised and exhausted, replied: 'Yes, I am a doctor. But I have no instruments or medicine here. I will do my best."

They took him to a separate room, where they had brought the sick guard lying on a straw bed. Edward examined him carefully, touching his forehead, looking at his symptoms. "He definitely has a fever," he noted, "But it may not be the plague. There are other diseases with similar symptoms."

"And what do you suggest?" asked Paul, hopeful.

Edward reflected for a moment. "I need herbs and boiling water. And a clean place to operate."

The guards, desperate, immediately agreed. Within hours, the room was transformed into a makeshift hospital. Some prisoners were involved in the search for herbs and the preparation of decoctions.

Edward's friend Thomas was called in to help. "What are you doing, Edward? This could be a trap," he whispered.

"I have no choice, Thomas," Edward replied. "If I can help, I have to. Maybe it will buy us some time."

As Edward worked beside the sick guard, trying to reduce the fever and calm the pain, the prisoners and guards began to see a light of hope. The animosity between them diminished and solidarity took over.

'If you get through this, I'll buy you a beer,' Paul said to his companion, trying to joke to relieve the tension. He smiled weakly. "I'll keep that in mind."

Days passed, and the guard slowly began to show signs of improvement. His fever diminished and his complexion returned to normal. The guards, grateful for Edward's assistance, treated him with renewed respect.

"You are a miracle worker," said Edward, smiling.

"Yes, thanks to you," the guard replied, his voice still weak but sincere. "You saved my life."

That single act of humanity had a profound impact on the prison. Prisoners and guards began to work together, trying to fight the disease together. Edward, with the help of Thomas, began to treat other patients, using his medical knowledge to help as many people as possible.

In the midst of the chaos and tragedy of the plague, the prison became a place of hope and solidarity. Compassion and humanity shone amidst the darkness, proving that even in the most desperate situations, love and care can make a difference.

The situation, for both the guard and the prisoners, had improved considerably and relations between Edward and his jailers had normalised to such an extent that they decided to let him leave with his friend Thomas.

In the Heart of Chaos

Cries of despair, death knells and smoke from the fires dominated the atmosphere of the city. Edward and Thomas, once through the heavy prison doors, found themselves in an apocalyptic scenario.

As they walked along the streets, they could see abandoned bodies, doors with a red cross painted on them, the sign of a plague-stricken house, and whole families in despair. But despite the panic and terror, a thin thread of hope and resilience still united the community.

"What shall we do now, Edward?" asked Thomas, trying to cover his mouth and nose with a handkerchief to protect himself from the stale air.

"We need to find shelter," Edward replied, "and then see if we can help in any way. My medical knowledge might be useful."

As they made their way through the multitude, a desperate cry caught their attention. A woman, with two children in tow, approached them. "Please help me," she pleaded. "My husband is sick and I don't know what to do."

Edward and Thomas exchanged a glance and decided to follow the woman. He led her into a small house with the windows barred and the door sealed with a red cross. Inside, a man lay on a bed, sweating and delirious.

"Could you do something?" the woman asked, her eyes shining with tears.

Edward examined the man, trying to establish the seriousness of the situation. "I need clean water and some herbs," he said. "We do our best."

Over the next few hours, Edward and Thomas worked tirelessly, treating not only the woman's husband, but also other sick people in the vicinity. News of their release and medical skills spread quickly, attracting an increasing number of people seeking help.

"I feel like we are making a difference," said Thomas, as he prepared a decoction with medicinal herbs. "But I don't know how much we can keep."

Edward nodded, looking out the window. "We are just two men against an unstoppable force. But we can't stop trying."

As the plague continued to claim victims, Edward and Thomas established a small health centre in an abandoned church. With the help of volunteers and survivors, they managed to organise a small relief team, distributing food, water and medicine.

"I never imagined we would become some kind of heroes," Thomas commented one evening as he sat down next to Edward, exhausted from fatigue.

Edward smiled faintly. "We are not heroes, Thomas. We are just men trying to do the right thing."

The chaos of the plague intensified, but Edward and Thomas continued to fight, offering hope and comfort to those in need. And, even in the midst of tragedy and death, their determination proved that humanity can shine even in the darkest hours.

The sun was setting, casting a glow on the crumbling walls of the church that Edward and Thomas had converted into a shelter for the sick. The crowds of people outside the church had been a constant over the past few days, but at this moment, there was a particular uproar. Among the crowd, a group of men on horseback led the way, and at their head was a smartly dressed man, though clearly in distress.

On his way out, Edward immediately recognised the pale face and distinctive features of the Count of Montegue. Although he had not had much interaction with him in the past, beyond that furtive encounter in the tavern, he was a man of great power and wealth, known for his lavish parties and influence in city politics.

"Count!" exclaimed Edward, approaching cautiously, "What brings you here?"

The Count, leaning on his steed, replied in a tired voice, "The plague, doctor. Like so many others, I too have fallen victim to this scourge. I have heard of your cures and hope you can help me."

Thomas, looking at the Earl suspiciously, murmured in Edward's ear, "We should be careful. This man has many enemies and I fear many friends as well."

Edward nodded, but replied, "Every life is precious, Thomas. Even yours."

They helped the Earl off the horse, led him inside the church, where a corner was quickly prepared for him. As Edward began the examination, the tension in the air was palpable. Many of the other patients and volunteers looked at the Count with a mixture of fear and respect.

"My symptoms started three days ago," the Count explained, "High fever, pains everywhere. I tried to treat it with my resources, but nothing worked."

Edward, touching the Count's sweaty forehead, said, "We will do our best, Count. But you must understand that this disease is insidious and unpredictable."

The Count, staring at Edward with burning eyes, replied: "I know you will do everything you can. I guarantee that if you cure me, I will be eternally grateful."

As the days passed, the Count's condition fluctuated. There were times when he seemed to be getting better, and others when his fever was rising dangerously. Edward and Thomas worked tirelessly, using every resource and knowledge at their disposal.

One night, while Edward was preparing a decoction of herbs, the Count, in a moment of lucidity, called Thomas to his side. "Sir Thomas," he said in a weak voice, "I know that you do not look kindly upon me. But I want you to know that, despite my past actions, I am grateful for what you are doing for me."

Thomas, surprised, replied: "Every man's life has value, Count. No matter who you are or what you have done."

The Count smiled slightly. "Perhaps after all this, we can start a new page. The plague has a strange ability to level everyone, nobles and peasants alike."

Edward, joining the conversation, added: "Illness makes no distinction, Count. But what really matters is how we respond to it."

As the days passed, miraculously, the Count began to show signs of recovery. His fever diminished and his strength slowly returned. When he was strong enough to stand up and walk, he thanked Edward and Thomas for everything they had done.

"Thanks to your efforts," he said, "I have a second chance in life. And I assure you that I will not waste it."

The Dark Mission of the Brotherhood

The city streets, once alive with commerce and laughter, were now dominated by a sinister silence. But in that silence, there was a persistent movement, a shadow moving from corner to corner. The Brotherhood of the Plague continued its mission undaunted, convinced of the rightness of its work.

The mercantile district, once the hub of the city's activity, had now become their favourite hunting ground. With the houses and shops abandoned, the Brotherhood had established a temporary headquarters in an old tavern, inside which they secretly gathered.

As the members discussed, a hooded figure entered the room, his step firm and sure. It was Richard, one of the leaders of the Brotherhood.

"We have a new list," he said, unrolling a piece of parchment. "They are the next nominees."

One member, his face concealed by a black mask, asked: "Are they all heretics and enemies of the cause?"

Richard replied coldly, "They are those whom the gods have appointed. It is not for us to ask."

Another figure, Seraphina, a woman with a sharp, confident tone of voice, stood up, 'It is time for our mission to be accomplished smoothly. We all know about the doctor and his friend. They must be eliminated."

A murmur of agreement ran through the room. The Brotherhood was well aware of Edward and Thomas' activities, and saw their intervention as a threat to their work.

Outside the tavern, the night sky was a clear, starry blanket, but in the streets, the fog thickened, hiding the Brotherhood's activities. Groups of two or three members moved quickly, penetrating the houses marked on the list, carrying out their mission with frightening precision.

In a house, an old woman was praying by candlelight when two figures sneaked in. Before she could react, she was overwhelmed. In another corner of the city, a young artist was dragged from his workshop, while his neighbours looked on helplessly, too terrified to intervene.

In the middle of the night, Seraphina and Richard stood on a rooftop, watching the city below them. "Look," whispered Richard, "what we are doing is for the good of all. Once we complete our mission, the plague will cease and the city will prosper again."

Seraphina replied in a thoughtful tone, "I really hope so. But sometimes I wonder if we are really acting by the will of the gods or our own."

Richard stared at her intently, "There is no time for doubt, Seraphina. The Brotherhood has a mission, and we will carry it out."

Meanwhile, in another part of the city, a small group of citizens, who had witnessed the Brotherhood's atrocities, gathered in secret, trying to find a way to stop them. "We have to warn Edward and Thomas," said one of them, "we know what they have done and what they have suffered are the only hope we have."

But the road ahead of them was uncertain. The Brotherhood was everywhere, and danger was around every corner. The city had become a playground for a struggle between good and evil, and only time would tell who would prevail.

The Return of Elize

The city streets were a bleak picture. Everywhere one looked, one saw mourning families and agonising sick people. The lanterns hanging in the windows revealed the spectre of death, the dark touch of the plague spreading incessantly.

Edward and Thomas were doing everything they could to cure the sick. The air was heavy and pervaded by the stench of illness, but the two men would not let it get them down. Their days were punctuated by constant calls for help and the routine of treatments.

On a scorching afternoon, while Edward was changing a young boy's bandages, Thomas' attention was drawn to a hooded figure slowly approaching the door. His path was uncertain, and he looked as if he might collapse at any moment.

"Edward," Thomas called in a trembling voice, pointing at the figure.

When the figure lowered her hood, their gazes met with two shining, feverish eyes. It was Elize.

Stunned and incredulous, Edward and Thomas ran towards her, supporting her as she collapsed in their arms. Her face, once pure beauty, was now stained with black pustules and signs of the plague. The disease had advanced with ferocity.

"Elize... Why did you come here?" murmured Edward, trying to hold back tears.

In a weak and trembling voice, Elize replied: 'I had no one else to turn to. I know what I did... and I deeply regret it. But now... I need your help."

Thomas, looking at her with a mixture of anger and pity, said: "After all you have done, you come here to ask for our help?"

Elize, with a remorseful look on her face, replied: "I know I don't deserve your forgiveness, but please don't let me die like this."

Edward, ever consistent with the compassionate doctor in him, took a deep breath and said, 'Every life has value, Elize. Yours too. We will do our best."

Elize, with her last remaining strength, tried to smile. "Thank you," she whispered, "Thank you for giving me a second chance."

Over the next few days, Edward and Thomas took care of Elize with all the love and attention they could give. Her condition, however, continued to worsen. But one night, as the city was shrouded in silence, Elize woke up, her eyes clear and bright.

"I feel that my time is near," he told Edward, "but I want you to know something. The Baron... intends to...". His voice grew fainter and fainter.

Edward looked at her intently, trying to understand her, "What do you want to tell me, Elize? What is the Baron's plan?"

But Elize, with the last remaining strength, only managed to whisper: 'Protect the city...'.

And with that, he closed his eyes for the last time.

Edward and Thomas, despite their grief and anger at Elize's betrayal, knew they had to act. The Baron's threat was real and imminent, and the city needed them more than ever.

Dusk was falling over the city, painting the streets in shades of dark blue and purple. The shadows of the houses seemed to lengthen, as if to shroud everything in mystery. However, inside the makeshift hospital, Elize's death had lit up the eyes of Edward and Thomas.

"We cannot wait any longer," Thomas exclaimed, staring at Elize's lifeless body. "We must act now."

Edward nodded, his eyes still shining. "He knew something, Thomas. Something the Brotherhood doesn't want us to find out."

The room, furnished with makeshift beds and shelves of medicines, vibrated with tension. The single lamp in one corner diffused a flickering light, casting shadows on the floor.

"We need information," Thomas said, quickly flipping through some notes on his desk. "And we need allies."

Edward lifted his gaze. "Do you know anyone we can trust?"

Thomas pondered for a moment, "There is a man, Alden, a merchant I met years ago. He is not of the Brotherhood, but he has many connections in the city. He could help us."

Without wasting any time, the two set off through the streets, trying to pass unnoticed among the shadows. The mercantile district, usually bustling and chaotic, was now ghostly and desolate because of the plague.

Alden's shop was at the end of an alley. A wooden sign creaked in the wind, depicting a golden scale. Thomas knocked three times, and the door was opened by an old but still strong man with grey hair and piercing eyes.

"Thomas! What an unexpected pleasure," Alden said with a smile. "And who is your friend?"

"This is Dr Edward," Thomas replied, "We need your help."

Alden let them in, and the shop turned out to be much more than just a shop. It was a veritable arsenal of information, with maps, letters and books scattered everywhere.

"The Brotherhood of the Plague," Edward began, "We've discovered things, Alden. They are sacrificing people, believing they are appeasing the fury of the gods and stopping the plague."

THE BROTHERHOOD OF THE PLAGUE

Alden nodded slowly, "I have heard of it. But it's much worse than you think."

As he spoke, Alden took out a roll of paper from one of the drawers and spread it out on the table. It showed a series of symbols, including the black rat with angel wings. "This is the sign of the Brotherhood, but it's not just a symbol. It is a map."

Edward and Thomas approached to better examine the drawing. "What does it mean?" asked Edward.

"They are secret passages," Alden replied, "that run through the entire city. The Brotherhood uses them to get around without being seen. And, I'm afraid, to target their victims."

Thomas looked infuriated. "We have to stop them, Alden. We cannot let more innocent people die."

Alden looked intensely at both of them. "I will help you. But you must be careful. The Brotherhood is powerful, and they will not hesitate to eliminate anyone who gets in their way."

With the map in hand and a trusted ally at their side, Edward and Thomas were ready to penetrate the maze of the city, ready to expose the Brotherhood and save as many innocents as possible.

THE BROTHERHOOD OF THE PLAGUE

The Labyrinth of Truth

The map, although ancient, was incredibly detailed. Streets, alleys, subways, and symbols indicating secret entrances and exits were plotted on it. Thomas and Edward studied every detail, trying to decipher the intricate passages. Alden, wearing a pair of thick-rimmed glasses, guided them through each section.

"The passages were initially dug for the sewage system," Alden explained, "But over time, the Brotherhood adapted them to their dark purposes."

Edward examined one of the symbols, "This seems to lead directly to the heart of the city, near the Baron's palace. Do you think it could be their main base?"

Alden nodded, "It is very likely. The Baron has always had close ties to the Brotherhood."

With a silent decision, the trio decided to start from that point. Advancing through the dark, damp cobbled streets, the atmosphere was tense. Every shadow seemed to conceal a danger, every noise alerted them.

They arrived at the entrance marked on the map, a wooden door hidden behind an old building. Thomas, with his military experience, listened carefully before slowly opening the door, revealing a spiral staircase leading to the underground depths.

The passages were damp and narrow, lit only by the torches they carried. Mould and cobwebs adorned the walls, and the air was thick and heavy. But as they made their way through, they began to notice signs of recent activity: torches still smouldering, fresh footprints, and a pungent smell in the air.

"We must be careful," whispered Thomas, "We are not alone down here."

Continuing to move cautiously, they arrived at a large underground hall with high ceilings supported by stone columns. In the centre, a large stone altar and around it, ceremonial masks and symbols of the Brotherhood adorned the walls.

Edward, with an expression of dismay, noticed a table near the altar. "Look," he whispered, pointing to a series of documents and maps. He approached slowly, scrolling quickly through the papers. "They are plans," he said, "They are planning another sacrifice. And this time it is something big." As they studied the documents, a noise behind them jolted them. A secret door opened, and a group of hooded Brotherhood men emerged, surrounding them.

Alden stepped back, while Thomas placed a hand on his sword. "You have discovered too much," said one of the hooded men, his voice cold and menacing.

"We will not let you stop the plans of the gods," said another, approaching with a shining dagger.

But before they could react, a loud noise came from another door. The entrance was smashed and a group of citizens, armed and threatening, burst into the room. It was clear that Alden had had the foresight to call for reinforcements.

A fierce battle ensued. Swords clashed, torches were thrown, and the echo of shouts echoed throughout the underground. But with the element of surprise and numbers on their side, the citizens managed to overwhelm the Brotherhood.

As the dust settled, Edward, Thomas and Alden found themselves surrounded by friendly and grateful faces. They had penetrated the heart of darkness and, with the help of the community, brought a glimmer of hope to a city shrouded in darkness. The battle against the Brotherhood had only just begun, but that day, they had won an important battle.

THE BROTHERHOOD OF THE PLAGUE

The Big Target

Hidden Discoveries

Edward and Thomas returned to the makeshift hospital, footsteps echoing on the wooden floors. The air was still impregnated with the penetrating smell of herbs and disinfectants. On a table in the centre of the room, a series of ampoules and vials bore witness to Edward's attempts to formulate a remedy against the plague.

Edward and Thomas had taken a number of documents from the basement, which they were now analysing.

"These documents... could be the key to everything, the irrefutable proof of the crimes committed." murmured Edward, unfolding one of them on the table. The paper was old and stained, but the words were still legible.

THE BROTHERHOOD OF THE PLAGUE

Thomas approached, examining the text. "This looks like a register of some kind. See, there are names, dates and next to... symbols. Perhaps they indicate who was... sacrificed?"

Edward nodded slowly. "And look here," he pointed to a passage written in darker ink, "It talks about a ritual. About how the sacrifice of certain people could 'appease the gods' and stop the plague."

Thomas flipped through another document, discovering intricate drawings. "These look like patterns of some kind. Perhaps they indicate specific locations in the city where rituals take place."

An hour passed quickly as the two men immersed themselves in reading and analysing the documents. At one point, Edward looked up, his eyes full of anger and determination. "They used the plague as a cover. Sacrificing innocent people, passing it off as divine intervention. We can't allow that."

Thomas agreed. "We have to stop them, Edward. And with these documents, we now have the evidence to do so."

As they were discussing their plan of action, the door to the study burst open. Agatha, a nurse who worked with them, hurried in, her gaze worried. "I came as soon as I heard you were back. Are you well? Is there any news?"

Edward showed her the documents, quickly explaining what they had discovered. Agatha listened attentively, her gaze increasingly alarmed. "We must inform the Lord Mayor (that was how the highest municipal authority was called) and the authorities, (although it was known that King Charles II had fled to the country to escape the epidemic and the Archbishop of Canterbury had remained in the city to somehow meet the needs of the city). With this evidence, we can expose the Brotherhood and stop these needless sacrifices."

But Thomas shook his head. "We can't trust anyone, at least not yet. The Brotherhood has its spies everywhere, even in the Lord Mayor's palace."

Edward nodded. "He is right, Agatha. We must move carefully. But first, we must protect these documents. They are our best hope of obtaining justice and exposing the truth."

Dark Plan

As Edward was arranging the documents, one of them caught his eye because of a peculiar seal. It looked heavier, written in black ink on thicker-than-normal parchment. He took it in his hand, scrolling through the words. With each sentence he read, his face paled.

Thomas, seeing Edward's reaction, quickly approached. "What is it? What have you found?"

"It is a plan," Edward replied in a trembling voice, "A plan to assassinate the Lord Mayor."

Agatha approached, looking at the document. "But why? What threat could it pose to the Brotherhood?"

Edward pointed to a section of the document. "It seems the Lord Mayor is suspicious of the Brotherhood's activities and is secretly investigating. They want to eliminate him before he discovers the truth and exposes them."

Thomas clutched the document in his hands. "We have little time. The assassination is planned for tomorrow night, during the banquet at the town hall."

The three looked at each other, realising the gravity of the situation. Not only did they have to expose the Brotherhood, but now they also had to save the Lord Mayor's life.

Edward stood up. "We have to warn him. We cannot risk the plan succeeding."

Agatha nodded. 'You are right, but as you said, we must be careful. The Brotherhood has spies everywhere, even among the Lord Mayor's servants. If they find out we know about their plan, they might anticipate the assassination."

Thomas reflected for a moment. "A distraction. If we can create a distraction during the banquet, it might give us enough time to alert the Lord Mayor and stop the assassin."

Edward approved with a nod. "It's a good plan. Agatha, can you help us get some... special ingredients?"

Agatha smiles, "Sure, I know a few ways to create some chaos."

Preparations began immediately. While Agatha headed for the larder to retrieve some herbs and ingredients, Edward and Thomas devised a plan to infiltrate the Lord Mayor's palace.

That night, as the city was shrouded in darkness and silence, the trio sneaked towards the palace. With the cover of night and dressed as servants, they entered without arousing suspicion.

The room was lit by candles and laughter and music filled the air, a rather strange, unusual and inappropriate scene compared to what was happening in the city. But beneath the festive surface, a deadly danger was about to be unleashed.

In the great hall of the municipal palace, the banquet was in full swing. Tables were laid, glassware glittered and candles diffused a warm, golden light. Nobles and aristocrats of all ranks were socialising, laughing and toasting their successes. The music of a string quartet permeated the air, mingling with the laughter and chatter.

In the middle of the hall, on a raised podium, sat the Lord Mayor, an imposing man with a long blue velvet cloak and a gold chain around his neck symbolising his position. Around him, councillors and dignitaries spoke to him, trying to attract his attention.

While the hall was enveloped in a festive atmosphere, Edward and Thomas, dressed as servants, moved stealthily through the crowd. Every step, every glance was calculated. They had to reach the Lord Mayor without arousing suspicion.

Edward whispered to Thomas, "We must approach him without alarming the guards. We use the cart with the drinks as cover."

With the trolley as a shield, the two started moving towards the podium, offering drinks to the guests. From time to time, they cast a furtive glance towards the Lord Mayor, trying to spot the right moment to approach.

Suddenly, a loud crash of broken dishes from across the room distracted everyone's attention. It was the perfect distraction.

"We are almost there," whispered Thomas, as he pushed the trolley closer to the podium.

Edward nodded, staring at the Lord Mayor. "Wait for my signal."

The Lord Mayor seemed slightly irritated by the confusion, but continued talking to his advisors, unaware of the impending danger.

"Now!" whispered Edward.

Abandoning the cart, Edward and Thomas quickly approached the podium, bowing in a respectful bow before the Lord Mayor.

"Well? What do you want?" asked the Lord Mayor, looking at them with surprise.

Edward took a deep breath. "My lord, we know this may sound strange, but we have come here to warn you. There is a plot to kill you this evening."

The Lord Mayor stared at them, trying to see if they were joking. "Who would you be to warn me of such danger?"

Thomas replied promptly, "We are allies of justice, my lord. We have discovered the Plague Brotherhood's plan and we know they want to kill you."

The Lord Mayor's face became serious. "The Brotherhood? I had heard rumours, but I didn't think they were real."

Edward nodded. "They are very real, my lord, and they are determined to carry out their plan. You must be careful."

One of the Lord Mayor's advisers, a thin man with thick glasses, interrupted. "And why should we believe you? You may be traitors yourselves."

Thomas replied firmly. 'We have evidence, documents that prove the plot. But now is not the time to argue. You must put yourself in safety."

The Lord Mayor looked conflicted. After a few seconds of reflection, he said, 'All right. I will follow you. But if this is a joke, you will pay the consequences."

Edward and Thomas nodded, leading the Lord Mayor out of the room, away from danger.

The room in which Edward, Thomas and the Lord Mayor took refuge was a small library, with shelves full of old books. The walls were lined with dark wood, and in the centre stood a large inlaid oak desk. A single oil lamp cast a shadow on the ceiling, creating an intimate and cosy atmosphere.

The Lord Mayor, still in shock at the revelations, sat down heavily in one of the leather armchairs. "So," he began, trying to regain his composure, "explain yourselves. Who are you and how did you discover this plot?"

Edward took a deep breath of air. "My lord, I am Edward, a doctor by profession, and this is Thomas, a former military man. We started investigating the Brotherhood of the Plague when we discovered they were behind certain obscene rituals and human sacrifices in the hope of stopping the plague."

Thomas unrolled some of the documents they had taken from the underground labyrinth and laid them on the desk. "We found these in the Brotherhood's hideout. They detail their plans and actions. And in one of them," he pointed with a trembling finger, "it clearly states that they wish to kill you."

The Lord Mayor leaned forward, scrutinising the documents. "But why? What is their purpose in wanting me dead?"

Edward replied, "They believe that by killing you, and putting one of their own in your place, they will have complete control of the city and be able to carry out their purification plan."

The Lord Mayor looked incredulous. 'Purification? What nonsense! The city is under siege by the plague and they talk of purification?"

Thomas nodded. "It is their foolish belief, my lord. They believe that by sacrificing the 'impure' and those they hold responsible for the plague, the gods will be appeased."

A heavy silence enveloped the room. The gravity of the situation was palpable.

After a long moment, the Lord Mayor spoke in a firm voice. "We must stop them. Not just for me, but for all the innocent people in this city."

Edward and Thomas nodded in agreement. "We need your help, my lord," Edward said. "With your resources and our knowledge, we can foil their plans and bring them to justice."

The Lord Mayor stood up, his imposing figure dominating the room. "Do what is necessary. You will have all my support. I will not allow these fanatics to destroy my city."

Meeting the Mystery

The heat of the room was oppressive, aggravated by the heavy curtains that filtered a dying light from outside. The crackling of flames in the fireplace was the only sound to break the silence that had fallen after the documents were revealed. The dust danced in floating golden spirals in the lamplight, like tiny spirits in an endless dance.

Edward glanced at Thomas, whose face was framed by a deep shadow, and took a deep breath of air before speaking. 'My lord, among the names we collected during our investigations, one recurred often. We wanted to know if you have ever heard of the Baron de Lacroix."

The Lord Mayor, who had so far maintained an imperial demeanour, showed a shadow of hesitation in his eyes. A brief pause of silence gave him time to regroup his thoughts. 'Lacroix? Yes, I have heard that name. He is a man of great influence and wealth, but very secretive. He recently bought a large estate on the outskirts of the city. Why do you ask about him?"

Thomas replied, "We are certain that the Baron is involved with the Brotherhood, perhaps even one of its leaders."

An expression of disbelief crossed the Lord Mayor's face. 'Lacroix? He is an aristocrat of great respect, with connections in courts all over Europe. Why would he have any involvement with a cult like this?"

Edward opened a small notebook, 'We have found traces of his operations in several of the places where the Brotherhood has operated. And there's more. Apparently, some members of the Brotherhood have been spotted on your estate. Moreover,

Thomas and I had the pleasure of being his, shall we say, unwilling guests."

The Lord Mayor massaged his temple with one hand. "This is a disturbing revelation. If what you say is true, the situation could be much more complicated than we thought."

Thomas leaned forward, his eyes intense. "We must investigate, my lord. Lacroix is involved as we know and could give us crucial information."

The Lord Mayor nodded slowly. 'If you decide to proceed, proceed with caution. Lacroix is a powerful and influential man. If he is really involved, he will certainly have resources and men at his disposal."

Edward stood up, determined. "We are prepared to take the risk, my lord. We must expose the Brotherhood and stop their plan, whatever the cost."

The Lord Mayor looked at the two men in front of him. 'I will give you all the support I can. If Lacroix is involved, we must find out. The city and its citizens depend on you."

Thomas thanked the Lord Mayor with a bow. "We are indebted to you, my lord. We will do everything in our power to protect the city and ... you, of course."

THE BROTHERHOOD OF THE PLAGUE

An Insidious Dinner

Edward's idea was bold, and like all bold ideas, it could easily fail if the slightest variable went wrong. He knew that pushing the Lord Mayor to the front line was risky, but the chance to expose the Baron and foil his plans made it a necessity.

"Lord Mayor," Edward began, his eyes staring intently into those of his interlocutor. "I know it is a lot to ask of you to act as bait, but if we could bring the Baron out of the shadows, we might finally discover his true intentions."

The Lord Mayor stared at his wine glass, the light from the fireplace reflected in his eyes. "You are asking me to put my life at risk, Edward. To use me as bait for a man who may be at the centre of this terrible conspiracy."

"I know, my lord," Thomas interrupted, "but without hard evidence against the Baron, we can do nothing. This may be our only opportunity to catch him in the act."

The Lord Mayor hesitated, struggling with the decision. "And if I accept, what do you propose?"

Edward drew a deep breath. 'Invite the Baron to a banquet here, at the palace. We will make sure that there are trusted people among the guests. If the Baron shows even the slightest sign of guilt or does anything suspicious, we will be there to stop him."

The Lord Mayor observed Edward and Thomas for a long moment. 'All right. I will organise the banquet. But you must ensure my safety and that of my guests."

"I promise, my lord," Edward replied with determination.

In the days that followed, news of the banquet spread like wildfire, and the anticipation was palpable throughout the city. On the day of the event, the Lord Mayor's palace was an explosion of colour and sound. Players played joyful melodies, while guests in sumptuous attire roamed the rooms, chatting and laughing.

Edward and Thomas, disguised as servants but away from the eyes of the guests so as not to be recognised, watched the Baron's every move from afar. The man, with his imposing figure and sharp gaze, moved with a grace that contrasted with his stature. He wore dark clothes, embroidered with gold threads, and a ring with a large ruby shone on his finger.

As the evening progressed, Edward noticed the Baron casting suspicious glances around the room. In a moment of the Lord Mayor's distraction, the Baron made a sign to one of his men, who approached him in a whisper.

"We are ready," whispered the man.

The Baron nodded. "Good. Proceed as planned."

Edward, having caught the interaction, approached Thomas. "Something is about to happen. We must be careful."

Shortly afterwards, one of the side doors opened and several men entered the room, all armed. The guests screamed and dispersed in panic.

The Lord Mayor, with surprising courage, stood up. "What does this mean, Lacroix?"

The Baron smiled evilly. "I am sorry, my lord, but I have other plans for this evening."

Edward and Thomas, hiding weapons under their servant's clothes, stepped forward, ready to protect the Lord Mayor at all costs.

"And who are you?" asked the Baron, scrutinising the two suspiciously.

"We are here to stop you," Edward replied firmly.

The Baron laughed. 'Still You ... are a curse and death is the only thing that can erase certain virtues. I should have made sure to finish you first. However ... do you think you can stop me with two swords? You are more stupid than I thought."

But before he could make a move, a thick net fell over him and his men, trapping them. From a side door, armed men of the Lord Mayor burst into the room, taking control of the situation.

The Lord Mayor approached the Baron, his gaze hard. "You had underestimated me, Lacroix."

The Baron, trapped and helpless, snorted angrily. "This will not change anything. The Brotherhood is bigger than me."

But Edward and Thomas knew they had gained a valuable advantage that night. With the Baron in custody, they finally had a hope of exposing and stopping the Brotherhood once and for all.

THE BROTHERHOOD OF THE PLAGUE

Surprise hit

Shadows in the Heart of the City

The sun was setting, dipping behind the buildings of that ancient, disease-torn city. The last rays of the sun were filtering through the stained glass windows of the makeshift hospital, a building that had once been a church and had now become a shelter for those stricken by the plague.

Upon entering, the air was thick with disinfectant and the penetrating smell of disease. People lay on makeshift beds, covered in sweat and with pleading eyes. Despite the turmoil and distress that permeated the atmosphere, there was a sense of unity and hope among the volunteers and medical staff.

Edward and Thomas walked quickly through the main area, waving to the volunteers they knew and offering words of comfort to the patients along the way. They found a secluded room upstairs, away from the misery and pain, and entered it. It was their office, where they kept medical supplies and discussed their plans.

Closing the door behind him, Thomas leaned heavily against it, letting out a deep sigh. "What just passed was too close an experience," he said, "But we cannot ignore the Baron's words."

Edward approached the window, staring at the city lit by torches and fires. "He is right," he replied. "The Brotherhood is clearly larger and more powerful than we had anticipated. The Baron's threats cannot be taken lightly."

Thomas moved to sit on one of the chairs, rubbing his temples. 'I wonder what he had meant? 'The Brotherhood is bigger than me'. Is this just an attempt to scare us or is there some truth in those words?"

Edward turned around, his eyes serious. "I think he wanted to tell us that even if we stop him, there are other members, perhaps more powerful, ready to carry out their plan. We must find out who they are and how to stop them."

There was a moment of silence as they both reflected on the weight of the Baron's words. The threat the Brotherhood posed was clearly much greater than they had ever imagined. 'Edward,' Thomas began, 'do you really think we can stop this Brotherhood on our own? We are just two men against a powerful and secretive organisation."

Edward looked at him, his expression determined. 'We are not alone, Thomas. We have the support of the Lord Mayor, and there are surely others in the city who do not want to see the Brotherhood triumph. We must join forces and stop them."

Thomas nodded slowly. "You are right. But first we have to find out who they are. The Baron was just the tip of the iceberg."

Edward approached the central table, where various documents and notes were scattered. "Let's start here. Let's see if there is any clue or information that can point us in the right direction."

The two men spent hours examining the documents, trying to connect the dots and unravel the Brotherhood's dark web.

Finally, as dawn began to light up the sky, Edward raised his head, the tiredness evident in his eyes. "Tomorrow we'll start looking for allies and information. The Brotherhood has played its move, now it's our turn."

The Unexpected Message

As Edward and Thomas were intent on discussing their next step, the sound of rushing footsteps in the lobby caught their attention. A young messenger, his face pulled and his eyes anxious, stopped in front of their door, knocking frantically. Thomas opened it quickly and the boy almost tripped as he entered the room.

"Gentlemen," he exhaled, trying to catch his breath, "I have been sent by Lord Mayor. He urgently needs you."

Edward jumped up. "What happened?"

The messenger focused his eyes, still full of terror. "Lord Mayor... Is not well. And he specifically asked for you."

Thomas's heart seemed to stop. "The plague? He contracted the plague?"

The messenger nodded slowly, his eyes shining. "I'm sorry, but I'm afraid so."

Edward grabbed his medical bag. "We must go immediately." Thomas nodded silently, grabbing his cloak.

As they rushed out of the room, the messenger led them through the deserted, dark streets of the city. Torchlight danced ominously on the facades of the buildings, casting twisted shadows. The city, once vibrant and lively, now looked like a tomb.

After a frantic run, they arrived in front of Lord Mayor's majestic mansion. Two guards stood in front of the entrance, their faces tense and pale under their helmets. Without wasting any time, the trio entered, being greeted by an elderly servant, his face marked with worry.

"Thank God you are here," sighed the servant, leading them quickly through the long corridors and up the stairs. "Our lord is in his room. I don't know what happened... he was fine this morning."

They arrived in front of a heavily carved door. Upon entering, the scene that presented itself before their eyes made them shudder. Lord Mayor lay on a large four-poster bed, his face sweaty and pale, breathing with difficulty.

Edward quickly approached, feeling the man's forehead. "It's very hot," he commented, taking a handkerchief and moistening it with water from a nearby vase, then passing it over Lord Mayor's forehead.

Thomas watched intently, his heart heavy. "Why him? He was one of the few allies we had..."

Lord Mayor weakly opened his eyes, staring at Edward. "Doctor..." he murmured in a feeble voice, "I... I need to speak to you.... private..."

Edward nodded to Thomas, who discreetly retired to the next room. He sat down beside the bed, his face serious. "Tell me, Lord Mayor, what can I do for you?"

Lord Mayor took a deep breath. "I know... I know what is happening to me, Doctor. But before I... leave, I need to tell you something... about the Brotherhood..."

Edward moved even closer, paying attention to the man's words.

"The Brotherhood... they have a plan... not just for the city, but for the whole country. They have powerful allies... "

THE BROTHERHOOD OF THE PLAGUE

Edward felt a knot in his throat. "Will you tell us who they are? We can still stop them."

With a last breath, Lord Mayor closed his eyes, leaving Edward with a huge weight on his shoulders. Leaving the room, Edward found Thomas, his face tense.

The Secret Behind the Ear

Thomas was arranging some herbs on the table when Edward entered the room, his face pale and his eyes clouded. There was an unexpected weight in the air, a feeling of gloomy doom.

"Thomas," Edward said in a broken voice, "Lord Mayor ... is dead."

Silence took over the room. Thomas slowly looked up, staring at Edward with incredulous eyes. "But... how? I thought it was the plague..."

Edward slowly shook his head. "I checked the body again. What I found... was not the plague."

They both quickly returned to the room where Lord Mayor's body lay. Edward, with trembling hands, lifted the man's head, revealing a small mark hidden behind his ear. It was a small wound, almost imperceptible, but Edward recognised it immediately.

"Snake blood," he murmured. "It is a rare and lethal poison. I have only seen this once, many years ago, in another country. It acts quickly and leaves very few marks."

Thomas looked at the mark with widened eyes. "But who could have? And why?"

Edward stood up slowly, looking around. "This was not a natural death. Someone inside Lord Mayor's mansion poisoned him. And I suspect it may have something to do with the Brotherhood."

Thomas's eyes hardened. "We have to find out who did this."

They both began to search the room, looking for any clue that might reveal the murderer. Thomas opened a small drawer on Lord Mayor's desk, finding a series of sealed letters. He quickly scanned through them, noticing that many were written in opaque black ink with an unknown seal.

"Look here," Thomas said, showing one of the letters to Edward. It was addressed to Lord Mayor from a certain 'M.D.', and spoke of an impending secret meeting at an inn on the outskirts of town.

Edward took one of the letters, noticing the same seal on the sealing wax. "This could be our killer," he murmured. "Or at least, someone who knew about the plan."

But as they scanned the room, a small vial fell from a hidden pocket of Lord Mayor's cloak. Edward picked it up, noticing the greenish liquid inside.

"This could be the poison," Edward said, cautiously sniffing the vial. "It has a peculiar, almost metallic smell. That confirms my suspicions."

Thomas looked at the vial with angry eyes. "Someone in here did this. And we have to find out who."

They both walked towards the door, determined to discover the murderer and bring him to justice.

Reflections among the Shadows of the Hospital

Inside the makeshift hospital, the atmosphere was tense and emotionally charged. Rough cloth curtains separated the beds, and the faint flickering of candles cast shadows on the walls

Entering a small adjoining room, used as a space for reflection and study, Thomas closed the door behind them. The room was sparsely furnished: a rough wooden table, a few chairs, and a bookcase overflowing with books and parchments. A single candelabra, placed on the table, emanated a warm, golden light.

Edward, his eyes still full of anger and shock, grabbed a chair and sat down heavily, resting his head in his hands. 'I can't believe we've come this far,' he muttered. "Poisoning the Lord Mayor... It is an act of such perfidy..."

Thomas, sitting opposite him, nodded slowly. 'They clearly want power at all costs. But we must be careful, Edward. We are now in his sights."

Edward lifted his gaze, staring at Thomas. "There is something that escapes us, something bigger than mere power games."

A long silence took possession of the room, broken only by the pattering of rain against the window. It was Thomas who broke the silence. "Do you remember that document we found in the underground labyrinth? The one that mentioned an ancient ritual?"

Edward nodded. "Yes, it was a cryptic reference to a 'hidden power'. But what could it mean?"

The soft glow of the candles still lit the room, but now on the table were scattered documents, maps and notes that Edward and Thomas had collected during their investigations. The atmosphere had become darker, as both were aware that their findings could lead to unimaginable revelations about the power and corruption that permeated the kingdom.

Edward, resting a finger on a map of the city, muttered, "It is clear that the Baron was not acting alone. The fraternity's power extends to many corners of the city, but I suspect there are hidden strings pulling the puppets elsewhere as well."

Thomas looked up from his papers. "You're right. And I think the key may lie right here in the royal court." He passed around a list of nobles and officials. "Look how many of them have had frequent contact with the Baron in recent months. It's not just a coincidence."

Edward looked at the list and nodded slowly. "It is as if a secret network has formed around the throne. But what could be the ultimate goal?"

Thomas shrugged his shoulders. "Power? Wealth? Absolute control? But it could also be something more... dark and sinister."

Edward rubbed his chin. "Have you ever heard of the 'Seal of Hebron'? There is a legend that whoever possesses that seal will have the power to command not only the kingdom, but also the dark forces. In ancient times, long before the kingdom was founded and castles rose above the mountains, there lived a powerful sorcerer named Hebron. Hebron was known not only for his ability to manipulate the natural world, but also for his wisdom. He lived in an inaccessible tower, erected on a mountain with a shimmering peak, where time seemed to stand still and the winds spoke in ancient tongues.

Hebron knew that its power was so great that it could fall into the wrong hands. Therefore, in a moment of deep meditation, he forged a seal, a small silver disc set with a rare black crystal, known as 'The Eye of Destiny'. This seal was the very essence of his power, concentrated in a tangible form. With the seal in the right hands, peace and prosperity would flourish; in the wrong hands, it would lead to destruction.

One night, a sibyl, wrapped in an ethereal cloak, visited Hebron in his tower. She whispered a prophecy to him: "The seal will be the desire of many, but only those who are pure of heart will be able to use it for good. When the sky cries fire and the shadows dance, the Seal of Hebron will determine the fate of the world."

Hebron, realising the gravity of the prophecy, hid the seal in a secret crypt, accessible only through riddles and trials that would challenge both the mind and the heart of anyone seeking to claim it. He created guardians, winged creatures with ruby eyes, to protect the crypt from intruders and evil-doers.

For centuries, the legend of the Seal of Hebron was passed down. Many sought to find it, attracted by its promised power, but few succeeded in passing the trials and riddles of Hebron. Those who failed were condemned to wander like restless spirits around the crypt, lamenting their fate.

Over the years, the legend merged with other stories and myths, and the precise location of the crypt became a mystery. But the hunger for power never subsided, and the seal became the obsession of kings and queens, magicians and warriors.

It was said that whoever possessed the Seal would have control not only over the forces of nature, but also over the dark forces capable of bending the will of men and changing the course of history. The promise of such power was an irresistible lure.

The legend took a dark turn when, in an age of conflict and greed, an evil sorcerer named Malagar sought the seal. He was said to have a pitch-black heart and eyes that burned with a green fire. With an army of shadow creatures, he began to search for the crypt.

After years of searching, Malagar reached the base of the mountain of Hebron. Using his dark magic, he faced each of the trials, sacrificing his creatures and even part of his soul to advance. But when he reached the final test, the Trial of the Heart, he failed miserably. The pure essence of the seal repelled his darkness, unleashing an explosion that destroyed much of the mountain and sealed the crypt forever.

After that event, the legend of the Seal of Hebron became a cautionary tale. However, for those who believed in purity and justice, it remained a symbol of hope, a promise that one day a hero might emerge, able to claim the seal and bring peace and prosperity to the kingdom. And so, the quest continued, fuelled by the flames of hope and ambition, waiting for the prophecy of the sibyl to come true."

Thomas blushed, "What a story! Fascinating and disturbing at the same time, So you think the fraternity has something to do with this legend? Are you suggesting that the brotherhood is looking for this seal? And that it has allies within the court?"

Edward nodded gravely. "If the brotherhood possessed the Seal of Hebron, they would have unparalleled power. We must make sure it doesn't fall into their hands."

Thomas rested his hands on the desk, thoughtful. "But how can we do that? And how can we find out who within the court is working with them?"

Edward pondered for a moment. "We should approach someone within the court, someone we trust, who can help us find out more."

Thomas brightened up. 'I have an idea. How about Lady Isabella? She has always been loyal to the king and has a vast network of contacts. She could help us."

Edward nodded, 'That's a very good idea. But we must be cautious. If it is suspected that we are seeking allies within the royal court, it could become even more dangerous."

Thomas sighed. 'I know it's risky. But we have to do something. We cannot simply stand by while the kingdom is destroyed from within."

Edward stood up and approached Thomas. "You are right. We must act, and we must act now. But we also have to be ready for whatever the fraternity has in store for us."

THE BROTHERHOOD OF THE PLAGUE

Talk in the Shadows

In a room of the castle, decorated with heavy tapestries and gold ornaments, Lady Isabella sat on an upholstered chair, her emerald green gown shining in the candlelight. Every detail of the room, from the golden candelabra to the works of art, showed the luxury and wealth of her family. The atmosphere was stuffy, heavy, as if the air was laden with expectation.

Thomas crossed the threshold, his uncertain step echoing on the marble floor. He felt the weight of Isabella's gaze, cold and penetrating, which seemed to read his soul.

"Lady Isabella," Thomas said with a bow. "Thank you for receiving me."

Isabella raised an eyebrow, scrutinising Thomas from top to bottom. "I was expecting someone else," she replied, her voice like ice. "But I guess you'll have to suffice."

Thomas swallowed, trying to hide his nervousness. "I come on behalf of Edward. We are concerned about the kingdom and wanted your opinion on some pressing matters."

Isabella slowly sipped her Tea, contrary to her manners, she offered nothing to Thomas and this could already give the weight and sign of Lady Isabella's attitudes and availability towards her guest, then she stared at Thomas with intensity. "And what do I care about the kingdom or what you or Edward think?"

Thomas took a deep breath. "The Baron de Lacroix and the Brotherhood of the Plague is a threat to us all. We have discovered that he has sinister intentions and..."

"I already know," Isabella interrupted, with a half-smile on her lips. "Do you perhaps think I live in a bubble? I am well aware of what is happening in the kingdom."

Thomas was surprised. "Then why don't you do anything? We can join forces and stop them."

Isabella laughed, a sound that echoed hollowly in the room. "And why should I help you? Why should I risk everything I have for a cause that may not succeed?"

Thomas tried to control his frustration. "Lady Isabella, many people have died because of the plague and the actions of the brotherhood. We must stop them before it is too late."

Isabella stood up and walked to a window, looking out. 'Look at the city, Thomas. Do you see how it burns? See how people are suffering? And you think I care?"

Thomas stepped forward, his voice trembling. "I don't understand. Why are you so detached? The brotherhood might want to take over the kingdom and you would be one of its first victims."

Isabella turned slowly, staring Thomas in the eyes. "I don't need you to tell me how to protect myself or my interests."

THE BROTHERHOOD OF THE PLAGUE

There was a tense moment, in which the air seemed to vibrate with unspoken emotions. Then Thomas spoke: 'I do not ask your help for me or for Edward. I ask your help for the kingdom, for the suffering people. If the brotherhood succeeds, all will be lost."

Isabella looked at him intensely. 'I have made my choice, Thomas. I have decided to protect myself and my family. If that means distancing myself from what happens outside, so be it."

Thomas nodded slowly, disappointed. "Thank you for your time, Lady Isabella."

Isabella smiled coldly. "Sometimes, Thomas, survival comes first."

With that final comment, Thomas withdrew, knowing that he would have to find another way to stop the brotherhood and save the kingdom. But as he left the castle, could not help but wonder if, after all, Lady Isabella was not just another piece in the complex puzzle of power and politics in the kingdom.

The sky was turning shades of orange and purple, and the sun was slowly setting behind the horizon. Thomas, with a hurried pace, made his way through the growing fog to the makeshift hospital where Edward was at work.

The interior of the hospital was lit only by a few torches and the dim light of a stove. It was full of beds with patients coughing and moaning, while a few nuns hurried from one bed to another, trying to comfort the sick. In the middle of the room, on a wooden table, Edward was intent on mixing some herbs in a bowl.

Thomas approached him, his expression tense. "Edward," he called in a low voice, trying not to disturb the sick people around them.

Edward looked up, his hands still at work. "Thomas, you're back. How did it go?"

Thomas hesitated a moment, then replied: "Not as I hoped."

Edward set the bowl aside and focused on Thomas. "Tell me."

Thomas took a deep breath. "Lady Isabella... she has changed. She used to be cold and aloof. She does not seem to care about what is happening in the city or the people who are suffering. She has made it clear to me that she will only protect herself and her family."

Edward was silent for a moment, digesting the news. "I'm sorry, Thomas. I had hoped that he might be able to help us."

Thomas looked at Edward with pleading eyes. "I tried, Edward. I tried to make her understand the importance of what we are doing, but she wouldn't listen."

Edward put a hand on Thomas's shoulder. "I know you did your best. It's not your fault."

Thomas lowered his gaze, visibly dejected. "What now? What do we do?"

Edward looked around, thinking. 'We must continue to do what we can. Help the sick, seek a cure and protect the kingdom. Even without Lady Isabella's help."

Thomas nodded slowly. "You're right. We can't stop now."

Edward smiled faintly. "We won't. We will continue to fight, no matter who is by our side."

THE BROTHERHOOD OF THE PLAGUE

The Great Fire

A Night of Confessions

The weight of the day was evident on Edward and Thomas' shoulders as they slowly made their way down the hospital corridor towards their respective rooms. The wooden floor creaked under their tired footsteps, and each torch on the wall cast shadows that seemed to dance in tune with the two men's troubled thoughts.

Arriving in front of Edward's door, Thomas hesitated, "Edward... May I come in for a moment?"

Edward looked at his friend, surprised, but nodded, "Sure." They both entered the room, a small space with a bed, a rickety desk, and a window through which the silvery moonlight filtered.

Thomas closed the door behind him and walked to the window, looking out. "It's amazing how, despite all that is happening, the moon is still shining as if nothing is happening."

Edward sat on the edge of the bed, looking at his friend. "Nature has a way of carrying on, regardless of human tragedies. Perhaps there is a lesson in that for us."

Thomas turned to Edward, his eyes full of sadness. "I wonder if we are making a difference, Edward. I have a feeling that for every life we save, a hundred more are lost."

Edward lowered his gaze, recognising the weight of those words. "I know, Thomas. I feel the same way. But we must continue to believe in our work. Even if we save only one life, that life has meaning, it has value."

Thomas walked over to the bed and sat down next to Edward. "I apologise if I sound despondent. But after the interview with Lady Isabella, everything seems so... desperate."

Edward put a hand on Thomas's shoulder. 'I don't blame you for feeling that way. I too have my moments of doubt. But we must remember that we are not alone in this struggle. We have each other and all those people out there who believe in us."

Thomas nodded, trying to hold back tears. "You are right. We have to be strong, not only for ourselves, but for everyone who depends on us."

There was a moment of silence, interrupted only by the distant sound of someone coughing in another room. Then Edward got up and walked over to the desk, picking up a small bottle. 'Here's something to help us sleep tonight,' he said, pouring some of the liquid into two glasses.

Thomas took one of the glasses and raised a toast. "Here's to hope. May it always shine, even in the darkest of times."

Edward raised his glass in response. "Here's to hope."

The two drank, and then Thomas got up to leave. "Thank you, Edward," he said. "For everything."

Edward nodded, "I thank you too, Thomas. We are a team. And together, we will get through this."

Thomas left the room, and Edward lay down on the bed, looking at the ceiling. Despite his tiredness, sleep was slow in coming. But he knew that, regardless of the challenges they would face the next day, he would not be alone. And with that reassuring certainty in his heart, he closed his eyes and let himself be transported to dreamland.

Fire in the Shadows

The darkness was deep and enveloping, broken only by the pale moonlight filtering through the windows. The hospital, once the centre of frenetic and chaotic activity, now lay immersed in silence, with only the occasional sound of a distant cough or the subdued sound of deep sleep.

From afar, however, a new sound began to grow, at first imperceptible, then increasingly clear. It was the rustle of stealthy footsteps, the breath of held breaths, the barely audible clink of armour. A group of men, hooded and dressed in black, moved through the darkness, advancing towards the hospital with sinister determination.

"Remember what I told you," whispered the leader of the group, a tall, imposing man with a scar across one eye. "I want no witnesses. Set the fire and leave. We won't have long to wait before everything goes up in flames."

His men nodded silently and separated, each with a torch in hand, looking for strategic points where they could set fire. With quick and precise movements, they closed the doors of the rooms where Edward and Thomas were sleeping, making sure they could not escape.

The fire crackled, flames began to bite the walls of the hospital, enveloping everything in a reddish glow. The acrid smell of smoke quickly spread, filling the air with a suffocating feeling of heat and danger.

In his room, Edward woke up with a cold shiver, even though the air around him was getting warmer. He coughed, trying to understand what was going on, and realised with horror that the room was full of smoke. He ran to the door, but it was blocked from the outside.

"Thomas!" he shouted, hoping his friend could hear. "Thomas, answer!"

Across the hall, Thomas was experiencing a similar situation. He had been awoken by the heat and light of the flames and quickly realised the danger. He rushed towards the window, hoping to escape from there, but it was too high to reach without someone's help.

Outside, the hooded men quickly retreated, watching with satisfaction as the hospital went up in flames. "Done," whispered the leader. "Let's go."

But as they walked away, a desperate cry stopped them. It was a woman, one of the hospital nurses, who had seen the flames and was trying to save who she could. "Help!" she shouted. "There's someone in there!"

The hooded men stopped, hesitant, but the leader made a firm gesture. "Leave her," he ordered. "We cannot afford to be discovered."

But they could not escape so easily. Other hospital residents were coming out, attracted by the smoke and flames. Seeing the hooded men, they began to charge at them, shouting and calling for help.

Inside, Edward was struggling with the door, trying to open it. But every effort proved hopeless.

The flames had now become a hellish monster, voraciously devouring everything in their path. The hospital, once a place of hope and healing, was now the scene of an atrocious tragedy.

Inside, patients, already weakened by their illnesses, were desperately struggling to save themselves. The nurses, their clothes caught in flames, tried to open the doors and windows, but many were blocked from the outside by hooded men. The air had become unbreathable, filled with thick, black smoke and the acrid smell of burning wood and fabric.

Edward and Thomas, locked in their rooms, had tried everything to escape. The two friends, having been through so many adventures together, were now facing a cruel and unjust death. The flames, unstoppable, had surrounded them.

"Thomas!" shouted Edward, his voice choked with smoke. "We must find a way out!"

Thomas, his figure visible only through the glow of the flames, replied in a trembling voice: "I tried the window, but it's too high. And the door... the door won't move."

Edward approached, his determination illuminated by the flames reflecting in his eyes. "We cannot give up now," he said forcefully. "We have faced so many dangers, we cannot let the fire overcome us."

But despite their efforts, the flames grew and the air was exhausted. Their strength began to fail, and the awareness of their imminent end became clearer and clearer.

"Edward," Thomas said in a faint voice, "I have always considered it an honour to know you and to work alongside you."

Edward, tears in his eyes, replied, "You too, my friend. We have done our best, and now, whatever happens, we will face it together."

The two ideally took each other by the hand, finding comfort in each other's presence. And as the flames advanced, the two friends heartened each other, ready to share their fate.

Outside, the scene was devastating. The hospital was engulfed in a gigantic blaze, and the cries of despair from inside made anyone in the vicinity shudder. Some villagers, awoken by the glow and smoke, tried to help as best they could, forming human chains to pass buckets of water and try to tame the flames.

"Who could have done such a thing?" cried a woman, her hands smeared with soot as she poured water on the fire.

"It must have been a deliberate attack!" exclaimed one man. "But who would have wanted to destroy the hospital?"

But despite their efforts, the fire was too powerful. The hospital was doomed.

At dawn, when the flames were finally extinguished, all that remained was a pile of smouldering rubble. The tragedy had claimed many victims, and the village was in mourning.

In the ruins, the bodies of Edward and Thomas were found in their rooms, a testimony to their unbreakable bond. The village mourned them as heroes, two men who had dedicated their lives to saving others, but who had now been unjustly torn from the world.

News of the fire and the death of the two doctors spread quickly through the kingdom, and soon the village was visited by nobles and dignitaries, who came to pay their respects to the fallen.

Lady Isabella, on hearing the news, was devastated. She had had disagreements with Thomas, but his death was too hard a blow to bear. With a heavy heart, she decided to give a generous donation for the rebuilding of the hospital.

But as the village tried to rebuild and move on, the question remained: who had started the fire? And why?

The answer to these questions remained a mystery, even King Charles II was informed during an audience in his castle.

The audience chamber of the royal castle was majestic and imposing, with tall marble pillars supporting the ceiling painted with depictions of past battles and triumphs. Vast tapestries adorned the walls, showing the royal family tree. In the centre of the room, on an elevated podium, stood a gleaming golden throne, where King Charles II sat. Dressed in sumptuous robes, his hands were adorned with rings set with precious stones, and on his head rested a golden crown.

Around him, lined up in a row, were the members of the court: nobles, councillors and dignitaries, dressed in sumptuous robes, conversing quietly amongst themselves. The air was filled with exotic scents, and the soft clinking of jewellery and armour filled the room.

A herald, in ceremonial dress, announced in a clear voice: "Bring forth the messenger!"

From the front door, a modestly dressed man, with a dirty robe and a face marked by fatigue, was led to the centre of the hall. He was Samuel, a messenger from the village of St George. He bowed deeply before the king and took a breath.

"Sire," Samuel began in a trembling voice, "I bring sad news from the village of St George."

King Charles II raised an eyebrow and asked in an authoritative voice: "Speak, messenger."

Samuel, trying to control his emotions, recounted the atrocious event. "St George's Hospital, founded by the noble doctors Edward and Thomas, was destroyed by fire. Many died, including the two founders themselves."

A murmur of dismay ran through the hall. Many nobles were aware of the hospital and its founders, and the news had shocked them.

"The fire...," Samuel continued, "was not an accident. It was set by hooded men. They closed the doors and windows, thus dooming everyone inside."

King Charles II rose from his throne, visibly shaken. "Who would dare commit such an act of evil in my kingdom?"

Lady Isabella, present in the crowd, her eyes shining, said: 'Sire, Edward and Thomas were dear friends. They had dedicated their lives to helping the less fortunate. I cannot believe anyone would have wanted to harm them."

The Duke of Worthington, an old man with a white beard and piercing eyes, intervened: "Sire, there are rumours that the Brotherhood may be involved. It is no secret that Edward and Thomas had many enemies among those who wished to maintain power over disease and cures."

The king, with a stern look, said: "If these rumours are true, the Brotherhood will pay for their treachery. No one dares challenge my authority and cause such destruction in my kingdom."

An advisor whispered in the king's ear: "Sire, we need to investigate. This tragedy may have much deeper ramifications than we imagine."

King Charles II nodded. "You are right, councillor. I order an immediate investigation. The truth must emerge, and those responsible must be punished."

THE BROTHERHOOD OF THE PLAGUE

The messenger Samuel, having delivered his message, bowed again. "Thank you, Sire, for your justice."

With a nod, the king replied: "Thank you, Samuel, for bringing this news. Go in peace."

As Samuel left the room, the tension was palpable. The tragic news had shaken the court deeply, and everyone knew that the consequences of this event would be significant.

At that moment, it was clear to everyone that the kingdom was about to go through turbulent times, and that the hunt for those responsible for the hospital fire would be at the centre of it all.

While the bulk of the court dispersed, a small circle of nobles retreated to a more secluded room. It was a dark room, with walls papered in deep red and paintings of ancestors peering down from above. Light came from burning torches placed on thin wrought-iron supports, whose flames flickered dancing and reflecting off the jewellery and ornaments of the nobles present.

Among them were the Earl of Ravenswood, Sir Reginald, Lady Eleanor and Lord Blackthorn. All were influential members of the court and, more secretly, of the Brotherhood.

"Wasn't the king's reaction predictable?" murmured Lady Eleanor, her face lit by the torchlight. "If he investigates too much we may all be found out!"

Sir Reginald, a man with a well-groomed beard, nodded. "Our mission is in danger. This incident at the hospital should have been handled more discreetly."

Lord Blackthorn, tall and thin, wearing a black robe and a ring shining on his finger, raised a hand in a sign of calm. 'You are all right to be concerned, but you must understand that the king had no choice but to respond that way in public. It is a matter of façade, of image. But in private? I doubt he will take further measures."

The Earl of Ravenswood, rubbed his beard thoughtfully. "How can you be so sure, Blackthorn?"

With a cunning smile, Lord Blackthorn replied: 'Why, dear Ravenswood, I have my sources within the King's chamber. While he speaks of justice and truth, he also knows that the Brotherhood has powerful allies and considerable resources. He too desires a 'purification' of the realm, though he will never openly admit to approving of us."

Lady Eleanor crossed her arms. "But what if these allies and resources were discovered? Edward and Thomas were close to unlocking many secrets before their... elimination."

"We need not worry about Edward and Thomas now," Lord Blackthorn replied. "Their tragic end only serves to strengthen our cause. And even if there are suspicions about us, we know how to handle them."

Sir Reginald sighed. "And the mission? Will we continue as planned?" "Absolutely," Lord Blackthorn confirmed. "The purification of the kingdom is essential. This is only a small obstacle in our path."

The Earl of Ravenswood nodded slowly. 'You are right. We have already done too much to stop now. But we must be careful."

Lady Eleanor added: "And we must also make sure there are no more surprises. I have heard rumours that there are others investigating us."

Lord Blackthorn nodded, 'I know. But I am prepared. The Brotherhood always has a plan. And, if necessary, others will have to be sacrificed to ensure the success of our mission."

As the nobles left the room, each knew that the path ahead would be arduous, dangers were always lurking, but they were determined to see it through to the end, whatever the cost. The Brotherhood was prepared to do whatever was necessary to ensure its rule over the kingdom.

Rebirth after the Storm

London was slowly being reborn from the ashes of devastation. Construction sites were everywhere, with the cries of workers and the sound of hammering echoing through the streets. The old hospital, once a hotbed of disease and death, now stood majestically, completely rebuilt. Its fresh, white stones were a tangible sign of the renewal that was taking place in the city.

However, not everything was as it seemed. Despite the apparent calm, beneath the surface, many families were still mourning their loved ones, victims of suspicious deaths. Many whispered that the Brotherhood was behind these deaths, but no one dared utter such an accusation aloud.

The streets of London were now full of life. The markets were crowded again, the stalls full of goods and the vendors were shouting out their offers. Children played in the streets, chasing balls and laughing happily, while women chatted among themselves, discussing the latest news.

In a crowded tavern, two men sat at a table in a dark corner. The atmosphere was lively, with laughter and song filling the air.

"I can't believe it's over," said the first man, a merchant named Geoffrey, as he sipped his beer. "I thought the plague would spell the end of London."

His friend, Robert, a blacksmith, nodded. "It is amazing how the city has managed to recover. But it is sad to think of all those we lost. Edward and Thomas, for example. They were true heroes."

Geoffrey nodded. "Yes, but you don't hear about them any more. It's like they've been forgotten."

"It's true," Robert replied. 'And about the Brotherhood, too. All those rumours, all those stories... and now? Silence."

Meanwhile, in the royal palace, King Charles II had returned to his beloved London. Sitting in his study, he reflected on the current situation of his kingdom.

"It is amazing how the city has managed to recover," he told a neighbouring councillor.

The councillor, Sir William, nodded. "Yes, but there have been many losses, Your Highness. And there are still many rumours about the Brotherhood and their activities."

The king sighed. 'Yes, I am aware of that. But now London needs peace and stability. We cannot afford to reopen old wounds."

Sir William hesitated for a moment. "What about Edward and Thomas? Many say they deserve to be remembered as heroes."

The king looked away. 'They were. But now we need to look forward. London must regenerate."

As life went on, and as London flourished, the secret of the Brotherhood remained hidden in the shadows. Rumours and suspicions would always exist, but the truth about their dark mission and the sacrifice of Edward and Thomas remained hidden, buried beneath the rubble of the past, as the city moved forward into an uncertain future.

THE BROTHERHOOD OF THE PLAGUE

Summary

Prologue 2
London 1665 3
   The Black Death 3
   Deserted London 5
Twenty suspects 8
   Introduction to Edward 8
   First Visit 11
   Rumours and Gossip 14
   Arrival at the House of Williams 17
   Macabre Discovery 19
   The Clue 22
   Doubts and Theories 24
   Search for Confirmations 27
The Sign of the Assassin 32
   Obsession 32
   The Unexpected Visit 34
   The Link 41
   Action Plan 43
   The Harrington Family 45
   The Trap 48
The discovery 56
   Gossip 56

- Infiltration 63
  - The list 69
- The meeting 72
  - Elize's advice 72
  - Comparison 75
  - Prisoners of the Baron 78
  - Betrayal 82
  - The City in the Grasp of the Plague 85
- The occasion 88
  - The plague arrives in prison 88
  - A Glimmer of Hope 90
  - In the Heart of Chaos 93
  - The Dark Mission of the Brotherhood 98
  - The Return of Elize 101
  - The Labyrinth of Truth 106
- The Big Target 109
  - Hidden Discoveries 109
  - Dark Plan 111
  - Meeting the Mystery 117
  - An Insidious Dinner 120
- Surprise hit 124
  - Shadows in the Heart of the City 124

    The Unexpected Message 126
    The Secret Behind the Ear 129
    Reflections among the Shadows of the Hospital 131
    Talk in the Shadows 137
The Great Fire 142
    A Night of Confessions 142
    Fire in the Shadows 144
    Rebirth after the Storm 154

Printed in Great Britain
by Amazon